# WAY ZARDS



## NEW BLOOD

J. E. Honey

TP

TotalRecall Publications, Inc.
1103 Middlecreek
Friendswood, Texas 77546
281-992-3131 281-482-5390 Fax
www.totalrecallpress.com



ISBN 978-1-59095-727-1
UPC 6-43977-75727-2

Printed in the United States of America with simultaneous printings in Australia, Canada, and United Kingdom.
FIRST EDITION
1 2 3 4 5 6 7 8 9 10

13th December 2011

***To all of those who never came back.***

And to two who did.
Brian & Jane
Thanking you for all
of your support, thank ya
kindly. You do not "HAVE"
to read it you know!

[signature] Great Uncle Jim

## About the Author

James Edward Honey has been involved in energy healing for close to 40 years. He writes in spite of obstacles with dyslexia and learning difficulties, which no amount of healing or wizards have been able to alter so far.

James's ambitions as a writer are to communicate, entertain, and give something back for what he has received. He is also interested in other things such as painting, drawing, and carving, not to mention his studies with various healing energies.

# About the Book

Fifteen wizards who live in a barren place need to find apprentices to pass on their knowledge of magic and wizardry to before they die. The first problem they face is remembering how to speak, as they currently use only telepathic communication. This gave me a fun way of introducing each of them and a glimpse into their characters.

They send out eight wizards into the world who each bring back an apprentice. One wizard notices that four of the candidates are female; this causes a discussion on the reasons why wizards have always been men and they have to change their rules. This created a way for me to look at the male and female differences real and imagined. Each apprentice has a form of communication problem, giving me an opportunity to explore the ways kids adapt to protect themselves from life experiences and different forms of abuse.

Each apprentice has to go before the higher council who has to decide if each of them have the right spirit, stamina, strength, and dedication to become wizards and to live in the middle of nowhere.

There is lots of problem solving that takes place as each group adapts to the other and to each other and we witness how each individual personality slowly unfolds. As the wizards have lived so long with only each other for company, they have all became more and more like each other and as things change so do they, each slowly becoming more of an individual.

# Acknowledgements

I wish to thank Tiffany Schneider for helping me with the birth of my writing and in doing everything that she could to help me take my first tentative crawl that led to staggering steps. Sue McCormack helped with the next couple of obstacles and later we were able to write a book together. Thank you, purple Sue! Thanks also to Ronald Zach for all his help.

I wish to thank Roy Edginton for his many years and ways that he supported me in many ways, especially with good pieces of advice that have proved so helpful ever since, not to mention being a role model, ta mate. I would like to thank Karen Janes for her many hours of reading and correcting so many of the early wizard drafts. Debbie also sends her thanks to her. I would like to thank Arletta Dylus for being the first person to be able to read the whole book that consisted of about the next six or seven of these: you really helped me, thank you. Thanks also for K.G. Bowden for redefining my short story until it became acceptable for him to publish it in his secret proceedings: thank you, Keith.

Huge thanks to Bruce Barstow, who was able to point out the path only because he had worked long and hard to make the road filled with his own kind of yellow bricks; he also owns a large chunk of Pearland! Thank you, Bruce!

Massive thanks to Anna Morgan for making the editing process easy and fluid, by her many visits to Pearland and the time she spent with each individual character.

I want to thank Bruce Moran for his faith, support, and many kind words that at times have been a real bridge from there to here, I appreciate them and you.

Finally, I wish to thank Angela, my partner and best friend who helped me make sense of the book and my life. Angela has read it, corrected it, made it better, helped me change it, only to have to read it all over again and again and then found others to help make it even better still. Angela, who has had the strength to say no, not just to me but to any wizard who gets out of hand while still maintaining a smile on her pretty face; Angela, who is 'the first' in my life in all ways and who has done so many things for the wizards that she is now an adopted wizard complete with a spelled room. Without her, this book would never have been seen and neither would the web site so if you like either of them then please join me in thanking her for their existence.

And finally, I would like to thank the people who have become known as the book club! They are Bruce & Christine Barstow, China Hunter, Karen Janes, Tiffany Schneider, and last but the one with the most experience and energy, Amelia Beamer. Thank you one and all, the wizards thank you as will the readers, ta friends.

# Table of Contents

# Prologue

Extract from Francis's book *The Wizards of Pearland: instead of a history-cum-diary-cum-forget-me-not notes and jottings (which you could call a prologue if you had the need).*

**The world of people was changing.**

*This was happening for many reasons, the main one being that there were now so many of them.*

Magic was less respected, as were the people who used it, and some did not even believe in it.

*This made the users uncomfortable around those who did not use magic or appreciate it.*

Therefore, the magic users found various ways to blend in, hide, or become a productive member of society so that they could practice their art in peace.

*Witches and Wiccans went underground; magicians became protectors or showmen, while the rest found somewhere to hide and to live in peace.*

Wizards became totally fed up and came together to find a place as far away from people as possible where they could wizard in peace.

*The wizards used spells to get everything they needed and had each other to talk to or to argue with. They were happy and content and they forgot about the world and what it might have been able to offer them - and the world mostly forgot about them.*

The wizards were always gaining knowledge.

*This was good because it was one of the best reasons to be a wizard, and besides, it kept them occupied.*

They eventually began to fight like a family who lived in too small a space. This was bad, and so they formed a council with the oldest and most talented wizard at the head who kept them from destroying each other or leaving.

After this most of them had the council to blame, so things became easier.

*They could then concentrate on wizardry, eating, learning, and doing whatever they wanted to do when and how it suited them.*

They were also getting older all of the time.

*This was acceptable - for everything eventually died - and as they lived a lot longer than most people they didn't really mind.*

But they had not had any apprentices for many years. The last few that had come to study wizard lore had not been able to learn their teachings, and none had come since the last one had left forty years earlier to become a glue salesperson.

*Now this was a disaster! When the last of the wizards died everything they had learnt and lived for would also die, and without wizards to wield magic and energy then it too might start to fade.*

Consequently, they had a problem that not even their combined wizard spells and energy could solve.

*They tried to ignore the problem (as most people do) until it got to the size where they either had to do something about it or move away from it. As they had nowhere else to move to, they had to face the fact that if they could not find anyone to carry on their ways then everything they held dear would eventually be lost....*

So when it became obvious to most of the wizards that they had a problem that needed solving and that it would not go away no matter how long they left it alone, the higher council finally decided to call a full wizard meeting to discuss the matter. They called upon every known fully paid up and fully-fledged wizard still living in the world to attend the meeting.

This was not a hard task for all of the remaining wizards had come together to share knowledge, magic, and gossip many years before; and, being wizards (and therefore lazy by nature) they had stayed together.

The other stipulation for attendance was that the wizards must have a least two of their faculties still in working order - oh, and they also had to be sane. When I say sane, I mean as sane as anybody who spends most of their lives studying rituals, learning strange chants, and ignoring most other things can be called sane.

This meeting contained all of the last known wizards who still drew breath, about fifteen in all.[1] These poor remaining wizards were the lost ones - not lost as in they did not know where they were (though there were days, I could tell you) - but lost as in they had nowhere to go and no one to pass on their knowledge to, and they were still getting older all of the time.

---

[1] I say about for it is very hard to count wizards, for each one goes a very long way.

# Introduction

The wizards found Jim when they were looking for someone to tell their story for them. As some of the council did not want their story told, and others would only consider a highly qualified writer, they discussed the matter as only they can. Finally they looked to see if they could find a writer who was good enough, and when they found no one, they looked slightly underneath their standards, then deeper and then deeper still. This meant that they made much ado of nothing, with many words and body movements. After some digging and discarding, they finally found Jim.

One of the subjects that was subjected to their arguing was the name of the person who was going to be writing them up!

Wizard Frank argued that the diminutive of James was Jam and not Jim. Wizard Arnold argued that Jam was a soft substance that oozed liquid, and Wizard Frank said that this suited this pseudo writer perfectly. So rather many wizards call him Jim and the rest Jam.

Jim, or Jam, writes in spite of obstacles with dyslexia, learning difficulties, and recalcitrant wizards.

# The Wizard Characters

## Jack:

Jack is the oldest and wisest wizard with the most experience of the art of wizardry, spells, and wizard rules. It was his idea to gather the wizards together and find a place where they could live in peace. He is now settee bound, and has not been observed standing for years. He spends much of his time asleep.

He is very small with thick white hair, moustache, and beard that lie around his face and head as in peace with the world. His eyes are a faded green although he usually only uses them one at a time.

## Roger:

Roger is the fattest, biggest, widest, largest and the most of any wizard in this story. This is of no importance except for identification purposes, as is his brushed back brown hair, trimmed neat beard or button nose. He is good, wise, and mostly balanced about things. He tries to do what he thinks is the best - primarily for the wizards - and then for everything else. He is second only to Jack in wisdom and the ability to clarify things.

## Arnold:

Arnold is small, thin, and covered in wrinkles. His tufted hair sticks out around patches of wrinkled skin. His beard is also sparse. He likes two things: best of all is ensuring he is first to arrive at any gathering or meeting. Secondly, he tells everyone that he was there first. He is wise and intelligent at his best, undermining and mean at his worst - especially when he is bored - particularly with Frank who always takes his bait (or does he just play along?) He gets bored easily and plays word games with Roger and anyone else he can, in order to fill up time.

## Francis:

Francis is the tallest wizard, and as he is skeletally thin he looks much taller than he actually is. He has dark eyes and no hair to speak of except for on the sides and back. He holds a lot of the old ways's knowledge and most of wizarding history within him; even though it appears there is no more room in him than, say, for a couple of broom handles. The rest of the information he keeps in books. He has a raggedy beard that stays that way due to his constant habit of pulling at it. He is vague at times and very insightful at others.

## Douglas Finwood:

Douglas is the only wizard to wear glasses - black rimmed after his old hero Buddy Holly. Douglas is the only one who has no beard or moustache of any kind, and likes to keep his red hair short and neat. He is very sensible and down to earth... for a wizard. He has a strong accent and no one is quite sure where it, or he, comes from as the accent is unusual and changes all of the time.

## Frank:

Frank is tall and thin with dark skin, black hair, beard, and moustache. He also has a dark brown voice. He sees himself as the speaker and moral keeper of all wizardom, even though no other wizard agrees with him. He has his ideas and considers the old ways to be the best - even though at the time he thought they were second best to the even older ways when he imagined things were perfect. He wants nothing to change for fear that he will not be able to cope. He gets straight to the point even when there isn't one.

## Colin:

Colin has a dirty brown beard and moustache with black hair. He is small and thin with a round head set onto a thin neck that looks too thin to support it. He looks almost boyish with his round head and large nose. He studies psychology... or sort of... nearly.

## Marcus:

Marcus is a very small, nervous, and insecure wizard who has dark eyes that can flash with frustration under his thick eyelashes. But usually they are just looking down at the ground. He has thick brown hair and an even thicker moustache and beard that are turning grey. He tends to agree with whatever is being said by everyone rather than offering his own views or disagreements. His speech is hesitant and always polite. Marcus found Tom, well, he met him and could not find a way to tell him to stop talking and following him around, so he brought him back to Pearland.

## Wilfred:

Wilfred is a small, thin wizard with thick yellowish-blonde hair, a moustache, and a yellow beard, a button nose, wide blue eyes, and an expression that is always very close to smiling. He is steady in his thinking and not liable to outbursts, but he can often worry a lot.

He is inquisitive, astute, and wise enough to know that he does not know everything and never will. This is unlike most other wizards who think that they either do know everything, or could if they just put their minds to it. He is sympathetic, listens, and learns (or as his pupil would say `that outer comes with a cushion'). He first used his spells to be able to speak kid-speak but soon became proficient in it. Wilfred found Gloria.

## Henry Darkmoore:

Henry is taller than Joe - but then who isn't? He has dark grey hair, beard, and moustache, and is slim rather than thin or skinny. He is what Arnold calls "lively" in his actions. This wizard really likes people and (even stranger for a wizard) likes spending time with non-wizards! He found Keryon.

## Bill:

Bill is solid, tall, and, in spite of his years, he is still physically strong. He has brown hair and light brown eyes but his beard and flowing moustache have gone white. He knows what is what (whatever that is) and is not above using his spells to make things happen and to make his life easier, and later the lives of his apprentices as well. His other main characteristic is that he adds "and that" to the ends of his sentences and sometimes the middles. This developed when he started speaking again - for he found that words alone did not seem to convey what he wanted to say so he added "and that" to the end of each sentence to imply that there should be more to fill out his sentences. This became a habit and one that he does not realise he is doing. He found Tara.

## Albert:

Albert is average in height, and podgy with pale, almost grey skin. He has thick brown hair, beard, and moustache that is going grey. He is always neatly trimmed and tidy.

He talks and grumbles to himself a great deal and is friendly to others.

He is the only wizard who needs to touch people to know what they are thinking and feeling. He found Mocker in the great forest.

## Joe:

Joe is the smallest of all of the wizards by a long way. He has a small thick body with a large head surrounded by his white hair, beard, and moustache. He is often at odds with things as they keep him away from doing what he wants at the time. He has darting grey eyes under a furrowed forehead hidden by his white hair that was parted on the left side then left alone to grow as it may - and it "mayed" quite a lot - all over his face and past his shoulders. Joe never mentions that he goes into town twice a week to eat in one of the cafés where he talks to many people. This would make his claim about disliking most people hard to defend if any of the wizards found out. Joe found the farmer Myrtle.

## Reginald:

Reginald is a small, solid old man, with a barrel chest, large belly, and skinny legs. He loves food and eats vast quantities of it. His nose looks as though he had left it somewhere and had finally found it under a table where it had been kicked around and stood on a fair few times. He has greasy white hair and beard with patches of less white. He talks softly with lots of "er"s and "um"s and the like scattered in his sentences. He found the boy known as the Mountain Boy.

## Martin:

Martin is large and comfortable (rather than fat) with wide-open eyes the colour of autumn leaves which match his remaining hair where it is not white or silver. He is amiable and easygoing in nature; and he is straightforward and very direct in all of his dealings. Martin travelled to the turreted city where he met a magician named Algernon Malkerith. He found Follia.

## Apprentices

### Gloria:

Gloria came from the school of learning where her mother had dumped her. She is small and thin with large dark brown eyes that show her intelligence. She wears overalls and boots, and has long unwashed hair dyed in various harsh colours. She speaks in her own "kid-speak" language.

### Tara:

Tara's parents sold her to the slave city of Varian when she stopped doing what they wanted her to do. She is blonde with blue eyes and fair skin and is much muscled. She maintains her muscles by exercising every day, as well as when she is bored or has nothing else to do.

### Keryon:

Keryon (pronounced either "keiron" or "ker-yon" or anything in between) is small, dark, and has wiry most things including a temper that he hides beneath a bored exterior - along with most of his other emotions and desires - especially from his friend, opponent, and hero, Henry.

### Mocker:

Mocker is small with brown hair, eyes, and often skin as well. He is intelligent and practical. He earned his name Mocker by mocking people, as being deaf, he can't hear them but wants to understand as much as possible.

### Mountain Boy:

Mountain Boy has fair hair, blue eyes, and is a very ragged individual. He talks in the way he imagines the knights of old talked, or way the old adventurers talked to their gods – ideas that he got from books.

### Follia:

Follia's parents abandoned her in an area of the castle city where all the unwanted children went. The other children bullied and neglected her because she was fat, had red hair, and was a handful. She is the youngest of them all by far and no more than a baby when she first arrives in Pearland.

## Farmers

### Tom Daunt:

Tom is very tall, the tallest person in the whole book and almost as thin as Francis... but not quite... though he is a lot taller. He has sticky out ears and brown hair that go along rather well with his brown eyes.

He never stops talking and has acquired the habit of adding an "a-" before words in his speech.

### Myrtle Houseleek/Daunt:

Myrtle is a farmer's daughter who is very tall and has wheat coloured hair; she is as strong as a bear and eats as much as a horse. She is not what anyone would call pretty; the best her parents could come up with was "homely." She is shy and a little unsure of herself but fiercely loyal.

# Chapter One: Things Change

If you go to the middle of nowhere you will find Pearland. In fact, if there were a contest for the most boring place on the planet then Pearland would be way up there with the winners. It is monotonous, dry, windy, and little grows in it beyond one tree and nine straggly bushes. There is nothing to look at - as in a mountain or even a hill - let alone a river or stream, and its flat surface is littered with nothing but stones.

This means that it has been completely ignored by everyone as it is of absolutely no use to them; which also meant that it was the ideal place for the last remaining wizards to come together to live in peace and isolation. There are fifteen wizards living there at the time of this writing, living underground in spelled rooms and eating spelled food and drink, leaving the place to continue to be one of the most boring places on the planet.

And it was here that Jack, the oldest, most experienced, wisest, and most powerful wizard, called all the wizards together to discuss their greatest problem… who they would pass on their wizard knowledge to before they all died out.

And so it was that on Pearland's wind-swept desolate plain, a group of wizards assembled; standing, except for two – one who sat on chair while the other lay on a settee – nodding in acknowledgment until one of them suggested that they should move into mass communication.

If someone had been watching this mass meeting of magic-filled minds, they would have seen many very old men standing, leaning, sitting, and in one case lying on a sort of settee all nodding silently to each other. Some had tall wooden staffs or small wizard wands with them.

Wizard staffs are long and thin but very strong and as tall as their owners (or even taller); they have runes carved into them and some have strangely carved tops in the shape of claws, or knobs or in one case a small fairy-type creature. Wizard wands, on the other hand, are wand-shaped, about one and a half wizard feet in length and can be hand held. These also have runes carved into them endowing them with power and character but being smaller, they are also easier to lose or forget about. The bigger and older staffs accumulate some of their owner's magical energy, until they form identities (of sorts), making them extremely hard to control - to the point where most wizards do not bother with them.

Most of these wizards had seats of some kind nearby in case they got tired; even those who were using their staffs to help keep them upright had a spelled chair ready. This standing, leaning, laying, lumpy collection of old men huddled in a circle and jostled each other with their eyes closed, nodding or shaking their hairy (or hairless) heads in silence, except for the odd moan, grunt, or sigh. Now, if this fictitious watching someone was also a wizard from some other place, say where they still had them, or if they had the ability to read mental wizard, then they still would not be able to understand much of their mind conversation. This was because this band of ageing seers had spent too much time together over too many years: like a family that chooses to stay together rather than going to all the bother of meeting new people and learning new ways. Consequently, they had learnt about each other inside and out, and so they were able to use many shortcuts in their conversations.

These mental communications included the odd phrase as well as images and feelings. The wizards made these into badly illustrated pictures, with words and feelings included from magical energies and spells, which they then sent into each other's minds. Now, what these strange ancient parochial gentlemen were discussing so intently in this unique way went something like this:

Wizard Arnold started by trying to depict his idea of *knowledge*: he made a picture of a wizard studying among many piles of books that are stacked up all around him. He tried to make the wizard look as if he had things on his mind by giving him a small mouth, square eyes, and many wrinkles on his forehead.

Wizard Roger looked at this image, nodded in appreciation, and tried to show *How hard won our lives have been!* He produced a picture of a sad tired little kitten that had lost its mother across which he sprinkled a layer of sad feelings.

Wizard Frank frowned at the kitten and then tried to make an image that represented his feelings of how he imagined a proud seer felt. It showed a Prophet who held in his right hand a wonderful secret knowledge while in the other it held a beautiful fish [2] (Frank could not draw babies

[2] This idea had happened when Frank was quite small and had overheard a joke about surrealists and misunderstood it. It went like this. How many surrealists does it take to change a light bulb? The answer was fish. The person who was listening to the joke said that they did not understand it and the person who was telling the joke explained that fish stands for everything in the surrealist world.

or knowledge but believed that fish represented everything that could not be explained). He finished it by making the figure slowly fade away in what he hoped was a dignified way.

Wizard Francis held back a tear at this last image, or where it had been, as he tried to make one that said *no one to receive our knowledge.* He created a tall thin wizard (who looked much like he did) standing on top of a mountain holding a rolled-up piece of paper in one hand and shading his eyes with the other while looking into the dark, distant, and cloud-swirling sunset.

Then Arnold made a picture that he thought said *no use.* The picture was of an empty, stained, and well-used plate.

Jack, the oldest wizard, attempted an image of *complete waste.* It was of a clean plate on a rack in a shop window with only a layer of dust for company and decoration.

Not to be outdone, Frank made a picture that showed (or tried to show) *pass on for others to build on.* This was a picture of an old wizard (beard to the ground) shaking the hand of a young wizard (small bushy beard) who is standing in line with hundreds of others behind him all smiling and saluting the old wizard with respect.

Francis, whose thoughts were wandering to his beloved books, glanced at the picture, then made one that showed a diagram of a stick figure with a pointy thing on its head.

Marcus, who was feeling uncomfortable as usual, tried to do *impossible.* The image was of a big, blank nothing.

Roger, ignoring Marcus, tried to make an image of *it's people we need.* The picture was of a group of matchstick people with round heads and no faces.

Martin, allowing his emotions to show, tried to imagine

his feelings of *all gone*. His picture was empty, filled with feelings of loss and dust settling on nothing.

Arnold made an agreeable face then tried to depict *then we need something to build on*. This picture was of a wizard talking to a pig that wore a wizard's hat that he was attempting to make into a wizard; the emotions that covered it were of despair.

Frank smiled as he tried to put across *unrealisable*. His picture was of the same pig flying in the sky and grinning down at the wizard who had taught him everything and who was waving his arms in disappointment.

Francis focused on the picture for a while, then nodded as he tried to show *always the way it has been*. His picture showed lines of wise-looking wizards stretching back into history. They were standing in rows and smiling out at the viewer, each holding one hand on the shoulder of an apprentice who, in turn, were looking up into the faces of each of their wonderful, kind, and gentle teachers.

Douglas tried his hand at showing *find nothing better*. His picture showed an evil-looking pig with a wizard hat on its head, a staff across its back, and a cigar in its mouth.

Henry sighed heavily then tried to show his feelings and thoughts of *waste*. The same pig was now digging a hole with its snout, while standing on the hat, the staff having fallen to the ground.

Arnold shook his head and made an image of *must find new people*: exactly the same image - only with a lot of dark blue despair - and a small stick figure in the left hand corner.

Colin blinked a couple of times to get rid of all the pigs, then produced a vision that showed many city folk in strange clothes all rushing around talking in a strange language. He added to this his feeling of sadness at the loss of a friend with a graph and a small pork pie in the left-hand corner.

Frank, who was starting to feel happy again now that things were looking bleak, tried to show *they are all too weak* by depicting a picture of a young man exploding.

Henry, feeling gloomy, tried to show his mood of *nobody is strong enough*. It was a picture of a single wizard looking sad with magic rushing out of him.

Colin, who had been studying the images as if he was looking for his lost keys, tried to depict his idea of *not the right type:* his first picture showed the city folk rushing around and then the young man exploding all over them and finally the pig fading away leaving only a steaming liver and bacon pie. There were loud sounds of lips being smacked until Roger put forward his picture of *all they see is what they can do with it*. It showed a young man with blank eyes waving a staff over the city folk with the feeling of abuse and misunderstanding pouring off him.

Francis nodded as he tried to depict his idea of *just as we did*: he showed them wizards' yearbooks going a very long way back in time and showing a faded photograph of them all (except for Marcus, who had not yet arrived in time for the photo).

Wizard Jack, who from his supine position was starting to get annoyed, muttered, "Nonsense." Then he tried to make it into an image that conveyed his thoughts as well as trying to change the collective mood. It showed a wizard with the combined history and magic behind him looking honourable with a glow above his head and looking to the future where the sun shone brightly.

Wizard Marcus did his best to show a *me*. His picture showed a younger Marcus arriving too late to be included in the yearbook with the feelings of it not being his fault splashed all over it.

Henry, who was trying to be honest as usual while not being seen as what he thought of as flash, tried to show a *they do not want to be us anymore* picture but he was having trouble with the best way to portray it. Finally, he made an image of a large chicken standing with its head held high and its eyes closed while at the same time pointing with one wing to show the bedraggled wizard which way to leave.

Albert nodded, wondering how long this was going to take, as he made his *that is right for them* picture that consisted of wizards on a higher plain to the rest of the world, and a soft feeling of superiority and righteousness, as they looked down on the fallen city folk far beneath them.

Roger sent his reaction to this by showing *we are no better*: the above images only with a much larger sneer on the face of the wizard and a smaller one on that of the chicken.

Arnold scratched his head as he sent his *right, we too only see what we want to see* image. He added to the above image the feeling that there is no 'right' - only differences and different interpretations - and then just for fun he added the feeling that the sky is about to fall.

Douglas, being more realistic than artistic, sent his *so what to do?* picture of a stick wizard shrugging his shoulders and scratching his head as he looks around at the aftermath of the faded and collapsed pictures of the last five images.

Francis stooped his shoulders as he sent his *no other way* picture of wizards through history passing on their knowledge, wisdom, and tips (like the best way to peel a mango - that kind of thing) to appreciatively smiling and eager apprentices.

Arnold shook his head as he sent his *lose knowledge* picture. This consisted of a feeling of loss and despair with a small feeling of wanting what the other person has but knowing that they will not get it.

Jack woke up, and seeing that nothing much had happened since he had fallen asleep sent an image of *options,* which became filled with all the options he could imagine - including two that suggested they eat another meal as soon as they could and then have a long nap.

Arnold, agreeing with Jack - especially about the sleeping part - sent or tried to send *we need to pass on what we have learnt and we need new blood to do it.* His image was of the wizards passing on their collected knowledge to fresh-faced, handsome young wizards and a smaller image in the left hand corner of the wizard cemetery.

Colin frowned in concentration as he tried to make his *we need somebody, but who, and where can we find people of the right calibre and type?* ideas and feelings into a picture. He ended up drawing a very large question mark with lines going away from it like the sun's rays.

Bill, who was feeling a bit sad, tried to depict his *always getting older* feelings by drawing an old sleeping cat and adding lots of feelings of always getting older but not really caring about it as there was always so much to do.

Francis, who was still thinking of his precious books, drew his *all this knowledge and we cannot find anyone who is willing or able to receive it* as a very dark pit that looked as if it went on seemingly forever; it had wisps of smoke spiralling upwards to join the dark purple and blue sky.

Roger snorted, then drew a huge pile of *Rubbish!*, adding a long feeling of complete disagreement and disdain with what had just been said, drawn, or suggested.

Arnold nodded as he tried to show *try harder*. He made a picture of what, in his estimation, were the very best bits about being a wizard. This included a mountain of confidence, as much food as you could eat, and a touch of wizard history thrown in for good measure. It also had a smudge mark high above the mountain (this was a mistake that he had tried to get rid of by rubbing it, and instead of getting rid of it all he had achieved was a dirty mark).

Wilfred, finally getting inspired, made an image as well as he could of *will is the tool*. His picture was of pure confidence coming out of a volcano that looked a bit like a tall, thin wizard dressed in a blue and a white robe.

Arnold, getting excited, added a very bright image of William Hugely (the wizard who put the 'wiz' into wizardry); he was looking up at the sky, smiling, and was surrounded by a feeling of total confidence and superiority.

*Not him... the other will,* Roger explained kindly, by making a picture of each wizard concentrating very hard on something in an attempt to show the idea of will. It looked like a bunch of stick wizards suffering from constipation.

Arnold, on getting the point in spite of the bad drawing, attempted an image that was meant to show *one last search*. It showed many wizards standing around, some shading their eyes with one hand, as they looked far into the distant horizon while others were searching far below them on the ground, looking under stones and behind bushes.

Jack agreed with the last image and made his *one more last attempt to save our kind* picture of lots of wizards going out into the world and talking to the people.

Albert, Reginald, Joe, and Marcus all reacted at the same time and in the same way. Their pictures were made up of a lot of large *UGHs*! One in bright colours with a dark orange sky for the backdrop; one had a white UGH! on a black background and another just had an UGH! made from indignant lines. The feelings they poured onto their images were of terror, dismay, and a very small one hiding like a petrified mouse.

Roger, who was already thinking about who would be the best wizards to send out into the world, made an image of a small bit of the orange backdrop - and the feeling of a frown that was turning into a hopeful smile - and something that looked like a squashed banana.

Reginald, after studying Roger's banana made a picture that said only one word, *ORANGE.*

*I like orange as a colour,* Roger replied (his picture showed a very wide feeling of defensiveness and rather a lot of orange).

Francis tried to depict *we must try for the sake of all of the wizards who have gone before us*. His picture showed a thin wizard surrounded by the feelings of hope and success with the added feeling that you were doing the right thing for every wizard who had ever lived and that they were somehow watching you and saying *what a good fellow you are*!

Jack agreed and tried to show *agreed* with a happy feeling of agreement - it had a small bacon sandwich in the top left hand corner and a mug of steaming tea underneath it.

Arnold, who was getting hungry, tried to show a *that's decided then!* image. It was the same as the one above only without the sandwich.

Roger tried to show *those who can, will seek* with a picture of the wizard council saying goodbye and good luck to the wizards who didn't have a good enough excuse not to go out and seek (such as they were not part of the higher council or did not move out of the way quickly enough).

Arnold made an image of *those who can, will seek, and those who are not able, for whatever reason, will prepare*. The picture showed the older members of the wizard council sitting and stroking their beards, thinking very hard about knowledgeable thoughts and, in the right hand corner, a frying pan cooking sizzling bacon.

Douglas showed he *agreed* with the feelings of ultimate agreement (or as far as a wizard can ultimately agree on or about anything).

Colin added his *agreed* showing more feelings of agreement and added a large dollop of *there is no other way to keep us in business*. He tried to change this on seeing as how it could confuse his fellow wizards, as they did not see what they did as a business but just a way of life. All he was able to do was to confuse those who were still looking at his image as he took some of it away and added other symbols.

Henry portrayed his *agreed* then added a green ditto showing a small left-handed ditto sitting on its own in the middle of the agreement lake.

Frank also *agreed* and made an image of a large blue feeling of agreement covered over with a thick helping of superior knowledge with a topping of *it won't work...* coming out of the lake.

Roger pictured his question of *any objectors?* It showed a picture of a wizard trying to hide behind something that was not adequate to hide all of him.

Then all of the wizards put together a picture of absolutely nothing that could possibly be seen as an objection in any shape or form with a white background that had no objection in its makeup.

Colin then asked something that he had been thinking about since they had all met in the flesh (which had not happened for a very long time). His question was *should we go back to using words?* His picture was of many wizards talking and waving their arms about and facing each other with their mouths moving slightly faster than their arms.

Frank, who was looking for anything that might be a problem, made a very large and defensive *Why?* picture of a very large and complicated why.

Colin, who had been rehearsing his answer, tried to show *psychology*. He produced a picture of many apprentices waiting for instruction. Then a very complicated object with a chart with lines going across it that no one looked close enough to see what was in each of the columns. Then just for good measure, he added that the chart was cross-indexed and highlighted into the bargain.

Frank, on not understanding what it meant, nodded as he constructed an image of *Oh, that stuff*. His image showed many people standing and nodding at each other.

Arnold, who also had no idea what Colin was saying, made an image of *he has a point.* This showed a picture of Colin holding a point.

Francis, who did not understand either, produced an image that tried to convey *they do have to be able to understand us.* This showed a whole bunch of young, eager apprentices looking intelligent, eager, and respectful, nodding their understanding.

Frank shrugged, then made an image of what he thought Francis had meant. He composed an image of *if we must.* This showed Frank talking about very interesting things to a group of interested wizards who all thought that he was the best thing ever.

Roger made a picture of *we must.* This showed many wizards actually doing things rather than just talking.

Jack sent out the words of *all agreed?* There was no picture as he was tired and thinking of other things, and as he knew that they knew that he was the senior wizard, they would all listen to him. Collective wizards all sent images of *agreed.* Some were more definite than others of course, but they all contributed.

Bill, who was ever the practical one, put his words of *So, we will go out to find some apprentices?* The picture showed lots of skinny wizards who were going out to do the seeking of apprentices, striding away into the sunset - with lots of hope and success all over it.

Nearly every wizard sent words or images that said *agreed.*

Roger, who was getting bored with it taking so long, made a picture of *now would be a good time to go out and try to find any young person that has the right spirit and correct personality.* The image was of lots of wizards doing things and finding young potential wizards each looking shiny and bright.

The remaining wizards sent pictures of agreement, a few sent more reluctant agreements and total agreement to the degree of worry by at least one wizard. Dominating the entire background were wavering backdrops of high hopes, warnings, optimism, excitement, ideas about apprentices, and one sausage roll.

The group of old men stepped back and reassembled into two factions, those who had 'volunteered' to do the seeking and those who were not going to do anything more than have a good nap or a cup of tea. Francis was planning to use his time to write up an interpretation of the meeting. He already had a title: "The full meeting of the wizards who came together to find a way for their combined knowledge and skills to survive into other generations for the good of all wizards past, present, and future." If he ever found further time, he wanted to alter it to something smaller.

The wizards who were going out to do the seeking turned to face a chosen direction where they hoped to find a human vessel that would be able and willing to begin the process of learning wizardry, and in so doing would save them from extinction. Then they slowly walked or shuffled away, eventually fading from sight, leaving just a handful of council members who stood (and in one case lay) waiting. They nodded good day to each other and then vanished one by one back to their comfortable rooms; all that is except for two of them.

One was small and thin with numerous wrinkles all over his body, especially his bald head and hairy face - this was Arnold. The other wizard was very, very large, wide, enormous even, as well as heavy, round, rotund, fat, and wobbly. He had the usual amount of hair and beard for a wizard - which is rather a lot. His name was Roger (named after his mother's older brother), and he frowned as he looked down at his companion before finally saying aloud, in a voice that squeaked from under-use, "So...." He swallowed, then tried again, "So... so... we should...

uhumm... use words now, Arnold. Er... do you remember how to?"

The smaller one arranged his wrinkles into that of a frowning face as he replied in a surprisingly deep and sombre voice. "Of course I do! It is you that I am wondering about."

They stood looking at each other and nodded for a moment, then wobbling his large head as he did so, Roger asked, "So... do you think any of them will find someone worthy of becoming an apprentice?"

Rearranging his features yet again, Arnold looked out into the horizon (as some of the better picture images had done) before replying. "I don't know. I only know that I hope that they do - for it is the only hope for our future. I do wonder if any of the people out there can still produce a child with the right spirit. I can only trust that they do. I also hope that they can be found."

Pursing his lips, Roger nodded his head – mainly to prove to himself that he had not forgotten how to purse his lips or nod his head - or indeed how to stop. He did this before saying through a sigh, "As do I, old friend... As do I. I wonder how they are doing?"

Shrugging his thin shoulders, Arnold replied, "I don't know... and neither do you. What I do know is that you and I standing around out here in the wind will not help them. So, Roger, I will see you later when they come back - with apprentices I hope. I know I've used up most of today's hope but let's desire that there will be something to see." With that he nodded and was gone - leaving Roger to stare up into the clear blue sky. Slowly shaking his head, he took a lungful of air and held it for a moment or two, then slowly exhaled it back from where he had taken it. Still shaking his head and wondering how the seekers were doing he disappeared, leaving only the wind to make any noise as it moved about the featureless landscape.

# Chapter Two: Marcus and Tom

In a place far away from Pearland along a dusty road came an empty wagon; empty that is, except for the horse that was pulling it and the three figures that it carried along within it. There was the driver, a round man with thick whiskers, careful eyes, and a button nose. The person sitting next to him was female. She was slightly less whiskery though much rounder and her eyes were just as careful as her husband's were. The last member of the trio lay in the back of the wagon. That is to say, most of him was in the wagon. His head and shoulders rose far above the seat behind his parents, while his long, thin body took up most of the length of the flat bed of the wagon, still leaving the end of his ankles and feet to protrude. This long thin boy sat, leant, and otherwise lay on the hard boards of the floor of the horse-drawn wagon quietly talking to himself. He was tall... no, taller than that... and he was as flexible and thin as an empty collapsed straw, only a lot taller.

Through the afternoon heat haze the driver saw a shape far ahead standing by the side of the road. It was on foot and wore some form of long garment that came to the ground. "Wht-at?" he asked his wife in his usual short form of language. He spoke as though every word cost him (or would cost him) an hour's wage, and so he kept his sentences to a minimum.

His robust wife, having gotten used to his ways many

years before, responded - as only certain story-book wives in the story-book world ever could - by saying, "Wha doo ya think I am, a keen-eyed a-gun toting a-pest shooting northerner or a-something? Ya think I can see a-better than you a-do, or is it a-too much for ya ta a-look? It ain't as if yee are a-saving your looks for a-something that yee have a-sent a-back East for ees it? Eets a-figure in a long a-garment with a long beard is awl that I a-can see as I a-suspect yee can a-too?" The husband nodded - to save on the money he would have to pay if they ever did decide to charge for words. He clicked his tongue to move the large horse from its lethargic walk into a more purposeful gait - just in case.

They were farmers, and all farmers in that part of the land lived by the rule of '*Just in case.*' This rule comes in handy when you want to do something that common sense would normally deny, like taking another drink to ward off the coming season when you have already drunk enough to fell a turkey and are facing ten miles across country in the rain or snow to get back to your farm. So '*Just in case*' means that you could have another one - *just in case* you might need it - or *just in case* it turns out to be your last drink ever and so you had better have it *just in case*. It also means that you can store more than you need, have another helping of dessert, put that cow to that bull, start the shearing later than usual, go to bed earlier, get up later, take a rest and a look around, and especially to have yet another drink. Then as you are having your one last drink, you can imagine the many things that could make your whole life much worse - *just in case* - making the drink even more valuable. *Just in case* also helps to cancel out logic, manners, the nagging of your spouse or mother, your conscience, parents, neighbours, good sense, and most other man-made concepts of control. All of which pale into insignificance by comparison with the *just in case* rule.

For *Just in Case = Pleasure without Guilt* - while indicating that there is a grain of logic and perhaps even a need for it somewhere, even if you cannot find it just at the moment. The best part of *Just in case* is that it can be adapted to cover all eventualities and desires, and the best part of that is that no one can criticise you, seeing as they use it almost as much as you do.

The creaking conveyance moved closer to the small, thin, nervous shape of Marcus, who was trying his best not to look like a wizard of any kind. This was the exact opposite of how he usually spent his time - doing his best to look and feel like a wizard, and failing. He was also thinking about his part in the meeting as well as how he had not been in the last Wizard Yearbook.

Marcus had been the last to become a wizard and the most recent wizard to arrive in Pearland. He was basically insecure by nature, and being the newest wizard added to this, making him always doubt what he was doing. He sighed and took a deep breath as he saw the wagon moving slowly towards him. Promising to do his best and not wanting to let himself (or especially the council) down he mentally prepared and tried to remember that he could talk again.

As the wagon drew even closer, the couple could see the figure was an old man with a long beard that was as washed and faded as his garments. The farmer's wife gave her husband a hint to slow down - *just in case* - by digging her elbow into his ample side. He gripped the reins slightly harder and wet his lips *just in case* he found the need to use them, if for instance he had no other option but to speak to this stranger. He need not have worried for his son took matters into his own hands.

Tom became aware that something different was happening by the change in motion of the wood under him. He squirmed around, and on seeing a stranger, called out to him, "Welcome a-there stranger, we wish ya well. Tom is ma name and these a-two fair a-folk are me ma and pa, Don and Matilda. We are the Dashes and we are on our a-way back from a-market after a-selling our…."

"TOM!"

The flow of his words were stopped suddenly by his mother who, fearing that he would tell the stranger that they had money with them, screeched his name before continuing in a more normal tone, "I reckons that this here a-stranger has a-more important things ta a-do then a-listen to your chatter there boy." She held the old man in the glare of her cold eyes, waiting for his reply and forbidding him to contradict anything she had said - or would say - in the future.

Marcus swallowed loudly then nodded his head as he asked in a timid, hesitant voice, "I... er... *gulp*... I would much appreciate a lift if... um... your fine steed could carry my extra weight?"

The air went colder around the couple as they sat watching the wizard as though he was going to do something they would not like.

Marcus read the energy that swam around them, which told him that they were afraid that he would try to rob them. "I mean you no harm or anything," he explained. He looked into the woman's eyes and blinked a few times. Finally realising her weakness, he continued, "I can of course pay you - for the privilege of such generosity - if that would... um... be acceptable."

The stern expression on the woman's face started to melt slightly at the word `pay' and her manner changed completely. She gave Marcus the smile she normally kept for formal dos and replied in a sweet but strained voice, "Why sir, our a-animal ees a-bred far carrying large loads end one a-extra person will nae even be a-noticed by him I'm a-sure." Wondering if this was enough 'manners' to give to a stranger who was going to give them money, she added, "So what a-brings yee ta this a-neck of the woods?"

Smiling nervously, Marcus wondered whether the woods had a body and a head to go with its neck as he replied, "I am... er... looking to see what I can see." Taking a coin out of the depths of his robe, he held it out to the couple not knowing to whom he should give it as he added, "I have been studying at one place for such a long time that anywhere that is not there will be a good destination for me." He smiled hopefully while feeling like a caught rabbit.

The farmer took the offered coin, gave it a long hard look, and putting the edge of it between his teeth he tried to bend it by twisting it with his hand. He nodded at his wife who took it from him and slipped it into her warm, waiting hand. As soon as possible, she would deposit it with the rest of the money they had made at market, far from the eyes of all but her husband (and only then when the moon reached certain angles and they had both shared a bottle of special corn brew).

Meanwhile, Tom had squirmed around until he was

kneeling on the wagon so that he could see what was happening. He stepped over the edge of the wagon without seeming to notice it, and walked towards Marcus. He stood in front of the wizard and looked down at him. It was in fact a very long downward look - have I said how tall he was? Then he escorted the old man to the back of the wagon where he helped him up onto its hard rough surface, carefully missing the tailgate that hung down over the end.

Thanking him, the wizard studied the tall thin youth who kept up a barrage of words and information, allowing only the most persistent of audiences to answer any of the many questions he threw into his sentences, mainly to make it seem as though it was a conversation. Tom spent a lot of his time listening to his mother telling him when to do things and when not to do things including, and especially, when not to speak. He also spent a lot of time alone with the animals or with his even quieter father, and so he was not used to either answers or conversations. Answers to him were like strangers, they were out there and he met them occasionally, but overall they were foreign and so he stayed away from them.

Marcus noticed that Tom had his mother's way of adding an extra "a-" to certain words for reasons he did not understand. Tom was saying, "Me folks have a-farm over a-yonder where they a-grow all kinds of produce and rear a-few mighty a-fine quality animals that do a-much of thee labour and the a-rest of them for eating. They teach me a-lot about farming but I ain't so sure I wus a-born ta be a farmer but I am nearly one so maybe I shud be. What do ye think? Not all folks a-can be a-farmers far there is not enough a-usable land, farmers is a-needed of course, for without them a-starve a-would we, for yee a-can not live on a-wild meat and a-berries can yee now? I a-wants ta be a farmer as its wot I knows a-best about and folks is always a-needed theem, but a-buying land is not a-cheap an I have a-nowt 'cept my savings an that would a-buy a goat at best and nae more so we a-will have to a-see wont we? Ye come afar? I have a-not yet a-travelled but one day I will a-go ta the four corners of thee a-world and see what I will a-see. I wants ta see them a-greet mountains and the a-greet seas an travel ta see if the a-tales I have heard is a-real or just a tale, what da you a-think - kin they really be a-true? I think they a-must be mostly a-true or why a-would folk a-go a-making them up? Once I a-broke me arm when a pig a-ran at me and a-knocked me over, it took forever to a-heal, and while it healed I a-had ta use just one a-hand to do ma work. I learnt a lot about a-pigs since a-then especially how not ta a get a-knocked down by 'em. Do ye know that every a-pig is different with its a-own a-likes and dislikes jeest like us? Pa a-taught me a-how ta recognize stock by theer a-shape and ta see at a-glance if it is a-healthy. Ma teaches me about thee a-chickens and even a-some letters, I knows a-lotta words and a-knows theem if they is a-big or a-small, I kin a-read a-nearly a long page...."

As Tom talked he waved his long arms around emphasizing his words, his hands flapping at the end of his wrists as though they were added as an afterthought. His eyes were on the horizon as he directed his words towards the great farm in the sky.

Glancing at the occupants in the front of the wagon, Marcus saw that Tom's mother was nodding her head in sleep, while his father made small sounds towards the huge horse (sounds that would be very cheap if he ever had to pay for them). In this way, the farmer kept himself awake and the animal moving through the warm afternoon heat that was becoming almost as full of Tom's words as Marcus's head was.

# Chapter Three: Wilfred and Gloria

In another part of the World and at about the same time that Marcus appeared by the roadside, another wizard materialized from nowhere. This one had blonde hair and eyebrows with a thick yellow beard and a nearly white moustache, and his clear blue eyes twinkled as he looked around him. He stood on a hill and smiled expectantly at the sight of a large town not far away. This town was very well known (throughout the places where it was known) for being a 'learning place of excellence' or 'knowledge centre'; some even called it a 'university' while most of the locals simply thought of it as 'that big place up yonder that teaches posh kids.' This large flat building was the ultimate in learning, or was where you sent your spoilt rich brats if you wanted them back at some point but not for a long while. Over many years the rich (and those who had enough money to impress other people with the same or even larger amounts of money) had sent their young to be filled with all kinds of knowledge, or indeed, just to get them out of the way. Within this fine building the masters had striven to teach these privileged children many, many subjects, from writing (joined up in class three) to geography of the known land and beyond; and, if you got to class nine, social standing (theirs, others, and especially how important their teachers were), to name but three. They also taught an appreciation for learning so that the privileged could tell their friends how important they were to have been taught by teachers of such great consequence. They learned everything from the fundamentals of mathematics to how to wash their hands after various activities. Those who had the ability or need, were taught religious studies, philosophy and their meaning in today's society (especially how important it is to send their own children to this school). Those who were not quite up to that were taught drawing, music, and how to jump up and down during various activities usually including some form of a ball. Then there was also needlework; hitting nails into pieces of wood; how to cook simple meals; and how to run around in circles for no apparent reason or, in the fine (or nearly fine) weather, across the country. If the student was not quite able to grasp any of these subjects then they learned how to apply pressure to a long stick held at two main points, one with each hand. When this was mastered, they then learned how to manipulate the stick so that the attachment at one end - be they bristles, strands of cloth or pieces of metal - would move about collecting dust and dirt, or spreading water or polish.

Three years earlier, the ruler of this seat of learning had something of a problem on his hands as the number of young (and the amount their parents were prepared to pay to keep them there) had been slowly dwindling. Student numbers had reached such a low level that some of the staff had been threatened, first with having to say what they did all day, and then with not being allowed to have so much freedom. It was even getting close to the point where some of them would not be allowed to stay and would even lose the money they were paid! A meeting was called for all those who had anything to do with the teaching, the running of the building, the cleaning of everything, the feeding and controlling of staff and students, and the repairing of what was damaged. Even the few random people who were always there (even though no one knew quite who they were or what they did) all attended. This collection of humanity filled the large assembly hall and some of the main corridors as well. As this was the most important and threatening thing ever to happen to them since joining this vast warm and safe institute, they were galvanized into taking direct action to be there. There were even some teachers among them that no one had ever seen before.

They put their collected hallowed, scholarly, accomplished, and educated heads together in an attempt to solve the problems of attracting new pupils, how to keep things going as they were or, if possible, how to make things better. How the upkeep of both themselves and the magnificent dwelling of learning they had all become so dependent on were to continue became the only thing worth thinking and talking about. After many hours of discussing, shouting, and interrupting each other, they finally agreed that they had to offer something that the parents would find attractive and beneficial to their offspring. The Master of Religions pointed out that his department gave the young the ability to understand (and misunderstand) how other people related to their gods and, more especially, how to appease the gods so that they could be safe from offence - and the odd lightning bolt. The Master of Sports suggested, in a superior voice, that if that was the case, then he should ask his gods to give them more money. The Master of Ancient Languages explained, in some detail, how his knowledge was at the heart of every language and without that knowledge, communication and understanding to any real degree were out of the question. He continued by explaining just how important the concept of personal growth was to everybody involved, within the ever-changing rules and oddities of the great outside. And that this was unachievable without his subject's input at the core; for without being able to use and show control over the various enounces then language would become nothing more than an animal grunt.

While the rest of the masters worked out what had just been said, the Master of Masters, the head of all of the masters (who thought of himself as the Master-Master of Masters), finally took to the stage. He had been waiting to see whether anybody had any suggestions that were any better than his and, on hearing that no one had, was now ready to give them his suggestions. This was Mr. Peter Alex Kendal Meatless. He was the boss, the governor, the man in charge, the one with all the qualifications, contacts, position, power, and authority to discharge any or all of the staff and make them do things they did not want to do. He stood smiling down at his audience knowing that he for one would always have a job. He wanted them to know this and he also wanted them to know that he knew that they knew.

He was the Master of Masters for many reasons, one being due to so many years of taking tests, and then learning how to pass even more tests. Then he had kept on doing so, passing so many that he had more certificates and letters after his name than any other two people put together. He had done this because he had no friends, and did not like animals or his family - and they also did not like him. In fact,

Peter did not really like most people. He had a brain that absorbed information and as it never changed, talked back, or asked for a reaction he had no reason to change; of course, he liked this more than anything else! He had no hobbies as such, other than telling others what to do.

Another reason he had been made the governor of the whole place was that his father had put in enough money to build a whole wing of the building - as a way to give this son something to do and get him out of the house (this wing was called the Meatless wing)

So Peter Meatless, along with the much sought after letters after his name that told everyone of his importance, stood looking across the hopeful faces beneath him. (His full title was: Master P.A.K. Meatless I.A.M. S.M.A.R.T.I.K.N.O.W. T.H I.N.G.S T.U.T.R. of O.V.E.R P.R.I.C.D.B R.A.Ts. He also had S.P.R.O.G.S. T.E.A.C.H.R as well as C.H.I.E.F. T.U.T.R., I.DID. I.T. and of course T.H.E. R.E.C.E.I.V.E.R. And lastly, I. A.M. B.E.S.T. S.O. T.H.E.R.E. He had other qualifications, but did not want to boast.) First, Peter asked the collection of teachers and staff just what the normal person (who could afford, and who would consider, sending their young to them) would think was important enough to pay vast amounts of cash for the privilege of learning. This caused another debate on the various real and imagined importance of each of their personal subjects and duties. Mrs. Delape, the Mistress of Philosophy, should have won it outright as she did most arguments, for she was very scary and talked about things that no one else knew, understood, or cared about. She threw her concepts at people as though they should be understood or they would come and bite you. But as the voices continued to argue, no one noticed that she had gone for a quick drink (only that they could say more than usual) and so by the time she arrived back they had moved on to other matters.

This discussion continued until the Master of Masters called for silence. Once this was achieved, with much help from the minders (who for once did mind), Peter Meatless proceeded to explain what he understood of the outside world and its workings. Most of the masters had been at this house of teaching for so long that they had lost any interest they had ever had in what happened anywhere else, including where their students came from or went to afterwards. Some had chosen their career to get away from the great out there and lived with a great fear of ever having to return. The few who still had memories of or contact with the rest of the world, and the population in general, agreed or mumbled disagreement with their leader as he talked.

"Good chosen helpers of the running of this fine institute, I have been researching into this subject and have come up with the following definitive observations." Peter Meatless paused just long enough to remind the gathering of his position by holding his head high and closing his eyes; then, holding the lapels of his handmade jacket, he told them, "There now seems to be many levels of society developing, and expectations amongst the populace are changing more than ever before. In society there are the lower orders of people who do what they can for as short a time as possible to enable them to procure enough money to do what they really want to do. Which, on the whole, seems to be finding ways of forgetting what they wanted the money for in the first place, and to forget what they had to do to earn the money in the second place."

It took a while for most of the audience to understand that he meant drinking themselves stupid; then as they explained what this meant to their colleagues, the rest of the staff nodded at his wise words.

"Many small communities that seem self-supporting, such as farmers, horse breeders and most traders or guild workers, have been happy to pass on their skills to their children, thus keeping the status quo. But now they are trying to improve their positions. They strive to get to a position where they can employ other people to make the humble or boring tasks bearable while they concentrate on selling their goods and impressing anyone they force to listen to them on the merits of their goods and skills. They are looking to help their children to step up in the eyes of the world and this is where we can help them!

"The ruler's dream of going to war with his or her neighbours is over, for the cost is inhibitory, to say nothing of the inconvenience to everyone involved. So the nobility now spend their time and money playing one-upmanship between themselves. This is their main objective, and sending their young to us is part of what they have always done. Now they have less money, and even less interest with anything outside of their futile circles, so we are getting less of them.

"Soldiers and warriors do not earn enough; neither do most villagers - so most of our pupils have up to now come mainly from the courts of the various provinces. This is not enough for us! They are producing fewer children. The fact that we have been offering the idea that by sending them here they will be kept away from other province children means now there are not enough of them to keep us going!"

He paused and leant his thin body forward then backwards as if he was weighing produce on his head; then, as he continued, he threw his hands open in front of him as if shooing pigeons with his fingers, "So, it is the traders we need to reach. Somehow, we must find reasons for them to send their young to us - they now have the money, and many, many children. All they need is the reason and motivation to send their children to us. Of course, we may lose some of the court people who will not want their precious offspring to be rubbing shoulders with common traders, but these traders breed far more often and have far more children so it would make no difference. If we could start a trend amongst these traders then the rest would follow, I am sure. That is how I see things."

There was silence until the Dean of Music jumped to his feet and clapped wildly. He was on the list to go and so was desperate, so nobody was surprised when he grinned and clapped wildly. The others who were on the short list also clapped and the Drama teacher actually cheered, but then he was the Drama teacher so everyone ignored him as usual.

After much intelligent discussion that took them nowhere as it usually did - especially if parties are of the same intelligence and are not being totally honest about what and why they are saying what they are - finally the Teacher of Basic Writing stood and waved his hand until enough people had noticed him. He raised his voice as if he was talking to his first year class, saying, "It seems to me that what is important to traders is learning how to make money and how to sell more of their goods."

Everyone fell silent, it was as if they had gone to lunch and found their plates empty, causing total silence and disbelief. Someone had hit the nail on the proverbial head. Peter Meatless was the first to recover, for he was not the Master of Masters for nothing. He nodded as he congratulated the teacher, whose name he did not know, "Thank you there, yes, thank you, I think you have some of the answer. We must offer them things that will help them in their everyday lives and perhaps even a little of how to enjoy the time when they are not working. Now, how do we achieve this?"

The Master of Mathematics and Common Numbers said that he could teach them how to count money, people, and goods instead of teaching subdividing atoms, and then pointed out that he would still like to explain atom subdividing, but only if there was time. The Drama teacher was so overcome that he stood on his chair and told them that he could teach them how to act and talk so that they could impress each other in many different ways. He added that he could maybe teach them some outdated manners if the Mistress of Human History would like to work with him. Everyone knew that he and Mary Bell, teacher of human history, had been working very closely together for a number of years, so this added task would affect neither their time nor activities in any way, as well as giving them something to talk about. Others came up with ingenious ways to impress the traders with costumes, rituals, verbal communications, and all sorts of improvements that as of yet, they did not know they needed. Over the next two hours they worked out a program to help the traders improve their techniques of moneymaking, talking in Traders (a language they would invent for them), fashion of different kinds, sports, and lots of differing entertainment befitting their class and outlook. They also drank a lot of tea and ate many biscuits, but then they always did that.

In the years following these implementations, every term more and more traders flocked to their palace of teaching excellence, and offered more and more money to take their various offspring as students. The fees doubled then doubled again, and as they did not want to appear money orientated (even though they were), the teachers made a rule that stated they would even take a percentage of the poorest traders's children who could not pay but had some ability to learn. These were often the only pupils who had any real ability or reason to learn. This was good for everyone concerned, and so the number of pupils - and the fees - went up accordingly.

It was to this newly painted and extended place of excellence that a blonde haired and yellow bearded wizard named Wilfred[3] came looking for a job. Well, he was not really looking for a job - but for an apprentice or two if he could find any - and he thought that this was the right approach. He was basically a nice man who tried to respect things as much as he could before his patience ran out. He was going through the process of applying for a teaching post as a way to get inside to meet the young people who lived there - instead of just spelling the information out of them as most of his fellow wizards would have done.

His interview commenced with the Master of Masters, who now carried a cane with a carved horse's head to show

[3] Remember him from the start of the chapter? It went like this: In another part of the world and at about the same time that Marcus appeared by the roadside, another wizard materialized from nowhere. This one had blonde hair and eyebrows with a thick yellow beard and a nearly white moustache, and his clear blue eyes twinkled as he looked around him.

anyone who could not tell from his walk and airs alone his true and exulted position in scholarly society. Peter Meatless and most of his letters started the interview for the post of part-time teacher. Looking superior and a bit stuck up, Peter asked, "So, you wish to teach within this prestigious house of learning, do you?"

"That would suit my purpose," Wilfred replied politely.

Pursing his lips, Peter looked the individual up and down, and thought, "Hmm... he is a bit old, but maybe that would mean he would cost less money." Then he added to his observations, "Mind you, he is also scruffy so he could not be expecting a large wage, and he looks like he had a brain at some time which might be of use. Also he would not get a job like this anywhere else so he would be very accommodating and not cause a fuss over his duties - especially his fees... hmm," he told himself then asked Wilfred, "Do you know anything about discipline?"

Wilfred remembered the many hours he had often spent sitting in cold, dark caves learning ancient words or hieroglyphic spells, then having to repeat them back in an attempt to affect some type of spirit or other force to manifest into his plane of existence and then to be able to control it with just his will power alone. "I think I know a little on the subject," he replied slowly.

Smiling and rubbing his hands together, the younger man replied, "Good - and a fine answer if I may say. Now, would you say that you know anything about the importance of memory?"

The hours he had spent learning the rituals eased the wizard's reply. "I believe so."

"Excellent!" Peter replied, forming his fingers into a spire (or roof support) as he glanced up at the ceiling, asking, "And what do you know about making money?"

Money to wizards was what the weather was to people who never left home - not really their concern or problem. If a wizard needed anything they just manifested it from the energy that was left lying around using spells, and if they needed money then it too was spelled. So he had to confess, "I know very little about money, I am afraid; it has not really concerned me."

Clapping his hands together the Master of Masters confided happily, "The last thing we need around here is somebody else who knows nothing but money making, or thinks they do. Right! You have the job, are you ready to start?"

The wizard nodded and stood up, frowning as Peter clapped him on the shoulder and used this contact point to pull and push him through the passages to where the problem classes were being taught (or not, depending on the resources and interest of those who were doing the teaching). Through his new spelled clothes, the wizard could feel the Master of Master's true feelings flowing from his hand as they walked past the many classrooms. Wilfred read the thoughts that were entwined in the energy that told him what Peter was thinking: "as long as this old man holds them for a day or so then most of the parents will have arrived to take the brats out of our hair. If he only lasts an hour it will still be beneficial... especially to Brian, who is still refusing to come down from the loft where he has barricaded himself after his last ordeal with them."

Peter Meatless led Wilfred through the many corridors until they came to a stop outside a faded green door through which a lot of noise was escaping, despite the door's best efforts to keep it on the other side. Flinching at an especially loud crashing noise and then grinning unconvincingly, the younger man gave Wilfred a last pat on the shoulder, smiled, and then hastened quickly away. Wilfred slowly opened the door and smiled happily to himself at the sight that confronted his old eyes.

As he opened the door wider, he told himself, "Well, if I can't find someone here amongst all this wild energy, then I don't know where else to look!" The noise continued as he stepped inside and looked around at the young people he was supposed to teach an undefined "something" to (if he survived long enough, that was).

Smiling, Wilfred entered the classroom fully, closed the door behind him and looked around at the pupils, some of whom were standing on desks and throwing things at each other in a casual manner. Two of them half sat and half lay together in one corner; they were folded around each other and appeared to be trying to get inside the other one's body via their mouths. A bunch of them sat in a corner smoking some herbal mixture that smelt vaguely of dried rose leaves, which produced a reddish smoke that wafted lazily up to the ceiling. Three were looking at a magazine and making grunting noises. Some sat looking at their hands or talking to each other and three were at the back of the class gesticulating wildly to each other. The rest of the pupils were shouting and screaming encouragement as they gathered around two combatants in another corner; they rolled on the filthy floor - hitting, scratching, and grunting insults at each other - while those who had formed a circle around them repeated the chant of "Fight! Fight! Fight!"

over and over, not even noticing that anyone had entered the room.

Wilfred went over his options, dismissing those that the other teachers had already used, such as trying to bully them, fool them into submission, or play some sort of social mind game on them. Shrugging at the waste of so much pure energy, the wizard shook his head making his long blonde hair do a wave dance around his skull. Then, making up his mind, he took a deep breath and waved his hands as he whispered a fire incantation, not forgetting the protection spell that would shield him from its effects. He had learned this protection spell fifty years before and he still kept the faint scars on his hands as a reminder to think before acting in this stupid way ever again.

From his fingers there suddenly spouted huge blue flames accompanied by even thicker blue smoke - much stronger than the smoke the young smokers had been using. The reddish smoke that was being produced by the herbal mixture looked once... then twice... and on seeing that it had met its match in the bluish wizard smoke, it ran away, escaping under the door as fast as it could flow - it knew when it was beaten.

The room slowly filled with thick blue smoke that the flames produced as they flickered around his hands. Soon every pair of eyes was on his hands and the fire that burnt around them, and for the first time that day there was total silence in the classroom. The silence was so complete that it even took the room a while to accept that the noise had stopped, and when it did it gave a good impression of a room smiling. Giving the command of resignation to his spell, Wilfred blinked the flames out of existence.

As the smoke reluctantly thinned a small high-pitched "Wicked!" could be heard somewhere in the crowd of youngsters who stared at him. The kindly wizard started to explain that it was not wicked, as the fire and smoke had no volition or personality of its own, and so it could be neither wicked nor good. Then he added that it really was more of a trick involving basic elemental control and a good memory for ancient language, not to mention a small amount of experience. The small dark-faced boy who had spoken waved his right hand in front of his own sweaty face as fast as he could which had the effect of making some of his fingers snap loudly against each other. Now that the boy had the old man's full attention, he explained that "wicked" was meant as a term of surprise, enjoyment, or joy.

Nodding, and wondering how he had done the finger-clicking thing, Wilfred used his foot to pull a chair to its intended upright position, and then sat down on it, showing the class that the flames had done him no harm by offering his hands out to them for inspection. As the youngsters gathered around to examine his hands, which the old man gladly allowed, he read their energy and desires. Soon he had enough knowledge to dismiss most of them as frustrated thieves and robbers, or what in his opinion was worse - business or society people. The exception to this was the two who had stayed at the back of the room.

He jumped onto the chair and asked the class what they all wanted from life and as they screamed their various answers at him, he half closed his eyes in the direction of the two who were of interest to him. "This won't do," he told himself, snapping his fingers loudly. He sighed in relief as complete silence rushed back - silently clapping its hands in joy to return to rule.

Every pupil became as still and quiet as statues. They were caught in the attitude of their last action by a stilling spell; as though they had ran out into a winter's day with too few clothes on and had encountered an unusual, quick, and total frost. Only the boy in green and white striped overalls and a girl with dirty multi-dyed sticking out hair could still move, even though they did not realise this fact until the strange new teacher spoke to them.

"Shall I repeat my question or do you need more time to consider?" he asked, moving slowly closer through the static pupils.

"Don't kill me!" screamed the boy, falling to the floor and covering his head with his hands before bursting into tears. The girl jumped forward to stand over him in a half-protective stance.

"Oh dear... dear me, I promise not to kill anything or anyone if I can find an alternative. Now, about my question... Ahh! I see...."

Peering down at the boy, Wilfred read the expanding energy that burst from his shivering body which told him that he would become an inventor of little worth (well, little worth to a wizard anyway - although to a purveyor of metal studs, or anyone who wore corsets, it would be of great worth). After freezing the boy, he turned his attention to the girl still standing over the boy with her hands on her hips.

"Some buzz boogie, how you freeze those dooks?" she said.

Blinking, Wilfred shook his head, wondering whether he had overdone the smoke. Finally, he realised that she had simply used her normal vocabulary - or what, to her, was a normal way of communication. So he used his wizard skills until he understood how her language worked; then, in a voice younger than his own and with words taken from her mind, he was able to ask her, "Spill me milk, chicklet, and sit on its top part." (Talk honestly to me, girl, so that we can achieve the very best form of balanced discussion possible)[4]. To his joy, she grinned and waved her clenched fist in the air in his general direction, telling him that he was "below normal temperature" (cool). She went on to explain that he had gained the highest respect of anything she had ever seen or imagined, or at least, since the last time she had used this particular phrase.

Wilfred formed a spell to make communication between them possible without having to take words from her mind, and in a voice even younger than before and much more excited than his last one he said, "Throw-catch verbal us" (Now we can communicate with each other). She gripped herself around the waist and rocked with pleasure, her long yellow, green, blue, pink, brown, and purple unwashed hair following her movements a couple of seconds later than the rest of her head, as if to prove that it too had real attitude. Watching her for a minute, he finally concluded that these actions indicated that she must be happy.

A short while later he went over their conversation in his mind to make sure that he had not missed anything. First, she had told him that she thought his actions were good and wondered how he had achieved them. Wilfred smiled at her as he told her, "You fables milk chick with open collection units. Splat place?" (You are an amazing young lady with a

---

[4] I have put translations in parentheses – to keep them safe.

capability to comprehend and remember many things. So, what would you like to do with your life?)

She studied him for some moments, during which time he allowed her to see as much of his energy and motives as she could. Then she nodded and revealed that she just wanted to go somewhere she could become herself, without the pressures that she was now under that forced her to have to hide a lot of her true self. Wilfred nodded, and told her that he had the ability to take her to a place where she might just be able to do that - and a whole lot more if she so desired.

She waved her head in his direction and told him that if his promise was real then she wanted to take him up on his offer. Wilfred nodded again, and then explained that he would first have to talk to her guardian, mother, or what not. She told him that she did not have a whatnot, but did have a mother who had sent her to this place to get rid of her. Wilfred informed her that if that was the case then the talk would not take long, and she half nodded as she told him that she hoped he was a "chain breaker" (someone who could free her from her bonds).

Just before the teachers and minders from the surrounding classrooms finally found the courage to investigate the lack of noise and the odd wisp of smoke that still escaped from under the door and out into the corridor, she told him, "I wanna swim with the little smoogs and fly with the tallest of the mostest mole cats. I am hot to wander there and back with my stick on my back and a wample in me filler." Wilfred slowly translated her words and discovered that "little smoogs" are a representation of freedom (as in fishes), as was flying. "Tallest" was best, and "mole cats" were children that could hide when necessary. She had therefore informed him that she would like to travel to find something worthwhile and that she needed to take very little with her except for her satchel, her wits, and her brain.

Stroking his beard, Wilfred grinned his triumph at finding someone with such potential and spirit. Then, as her concentration started to wander, he replied in his normal voice, "I cannot promise you that, young lady, but there will be more than enough to occupy one such as you, if, that is, you choose to follow me and put yourself up before the council?"

She frowned and put her hand over her eyes as she wondered what had happened to his voice.

Nodding in apology, he again adopted her vocabulary, explaining, "New droplet, if you line glue me to next there, we can open the wonder unused box, if ya old milker will unglue." He hoped that he had told her that she was able to go with him and discover whether she wanted to become an apprentice, if her mother would allow her to do so.

Grinning and waving her head around she informed him, "Scrumbled dirt piles I peeked out at Baby-dom. So need to refill me spark producer and use all of me head glue."

It took him some time to work out that she had agreed and wanted to be mentally taxed. He wondered if he would ever be able to understand her and communicate with her in his normal state of mind instead of relying on having to unravel her words or resort to spells. "Oh well, it's a small price to pay for one with such potential," he told himself, and then to the world in general he said, "Here we go then!

Do you have everything that you need?" He glanced at the young woman who frowned at him with her head to one side. He corrected his words again, saying to her, "Blank out and wheel our round bits and let's make new there as this is stiffer than the slab place, out shell us right?" (Or, as he hoped he had informed her, "Let's prepare our minds and bodies and leave here as this place does not have anything to teach you as it is as cold and un-stimulating as a morgue, so let us leave immediately.")

She moved next to him happily and the next second they were gone... a second after that they were back... to retrieve her "infill stuffer" (satchel). She squealed her pleasure in kid talk about being spelled away and back again as she grasped her satchel in her hands and explained to him what it contained and why it was important to her. Wilfred nodded, his blonde hair flopping across his face as he snapped his fingers to spell them away again.

When the door finally and very, very cautiously and slowly opened, the frozen pupils became normal, or as close to normal as they could ever get. The minders fell into the room, with the teachers close behind them, to find all the children screaming and shouting at the space where the old man had, just seconds before, been standing on a chair. They turned on the teachers and demanded that they bring him back as he was the sharpest thing since carbon-based utensils were introduced to any gleaming pre-young. (Wilfred was the most interesting person they had ever met since hands were given to young people who had not had the time to be corrupted by society).

Seconds later, Wilfred and the girl appeared outside the home that had abandoned her and which was filled with only bad memories. Wilfred glanced at the girl and asked her if she was sure. She nodded her head so hard he thought that she would hurt herself. Indicating that he believed her and that she could stop her head motion, he knocked loudly on the door. It was finally opened by a washed-out looking woman who took one look at her daughter and started screaming at her until she had run out of breath. When she had gained some more breath, she looked at Wilfred and demanded that he tell her what the little piece of doodle bat had done now.

Smiling, Wilfred informed her that she had actually done exceptionally well and had been moved into a position where she could learn many new skills. The mother told him that she had no more money to waste on the brat. Wilfred refrained from turning her into a cockroach at this, but instead told her that it would cost her nothing. Then, as he felt guilty about his desire to change her into an insect, he added that she would be paid - if that were acceptable.

Changing her whole manner, the woman smiled as she asked him how much. Wilfred spelled some money and gave it to her, then asked her to sign a piece of paper giving him complete guardianship over her child. Grabbing the money, she grinned and signed quickly, saying that her girl had always been a bit clever and that it obviously came from her side of the family.

Smiling, Wilfred looked at the signature and replied that he had no idea. Then he looked down at the child and asked if she needed anything from the house for her journey. The girl scowled at her mother hiding her true feelings as she replied, "I am slid free" (There is nothing here that I need).

Her mother started telling her daughter to say "thank

you," then stopped as she realised it was not her problem anymore. So she gripped the money to her chest, bid them a good day and closed the door in their faces.

Wilfred looked down at his chicklet and asked if she was ready.

The girl took one last look at the house where she had lived, then told him that she was "already there in head Dom with empty here" (I am already there in my head and have nothing to keep me here).

Wilfred put his hand on her thin shoulder and explained to her that they were going to a place called Pearland. She asked him why it was called Pearland, to which he confessed, "No one knows why it is called Pearland - there are not and have never been any pearls in it, on it or around it. Perhaps it was called this as some form of joke - if so it was so long ago it has ceased to be funny."

She grinned and told him that she liked it there already.

# Chapter Four: Bill and Tara

On the other side of the continent another apprentice-seeking wizard appeared. This one looked like most of the others except that he was fatter than some (Arnold, Frank, Wilfred, Jack, Marcus, Francis, Joe, Colin, and Douglas) and thinner than others (Roger, Martin, Albert, and Reginald) while being heavier, smaller, or leaner than the rest. The one thing he shared with them all was that he was a wizard and had passed all of the tests to prove it. Smiling to himself, as wizards tend to do, Bill glanced around, then started to hum quietly as he practiced some gentle light air magic as he strolled along the walkways above the slave pens of Varian. Bill had learnt that the great city of Varian was in the habit of stealing unsuspecting young people and keeping them as slaves. They had been doing this for many years and so he figured that if he were to find anyone who needed to find a new life then it would be here (or so he hoped).

These poor unfortunate people were kept healthy and well until they were damaged or got to an age where slave clients lost interest in them. What happened to them then he did not know, and did not really want to find out - for he might lose his temper and do something that he would later regret. He was here to find an apprentice and that was all; what happened to those who became old or ill he made sure he did not read from the energy that pulsed gently all around him. Even wizards cannot do everything - nor would they wish to - well, most of them anyway.

What he and most everybody else did know, was that the city sold (but mainly hired) these poor unfortunate people for various lengths of time to anyone who could pay. Most visitors came to the city only for this purpose: to hire a slave for a short time before they had to go back to their usual slave-less lives. This trade had started as a way to help the city to survive and save their economy from ruin. Now it had become their only means to continue to be one of the richest and most protected cities on the continent. Varian was one of the few provinces that still allowed the ownership of slaves, much to the happiness of the rich residents who ran the whole shebang and who benefited the most.

So anyone with money could hire a slave for a short time. During this time, they could do with them as they pleased - except to damage them permanently - all surface damage had to be paid for. This made the slaves very unhappy, angry, and/or despondent. It kept the city rich and caused the visitors to wear various disguises. As these unfortunate young slaves were stolen from far and wide, Bill reasoned that this would be the ideal place to find an apprentice. All he required was someone with the right spirit, who had the desire to find a new life. He gazed down at the listless bodies that sat or lay on the hard ground far below him in the slave pens. They were all dressed in loose garments with large numbers and symbols on them for identification purposes. To Bill they looked as if they were wearing cloth newspapers for the short-sighted. Bill studied each one, looking for that certain something that would make them stand out from the rest of their fellows. A *certain something* that meant that they wanted more from life and were not above putting up with old grey men and learning spells in various languages (most of which were dead ones) to become a wizard and gain the freedom that it offered.

After an hour of walking around the top of the pens studying the unfortunate prisoners, he had achieved two main objectives; first, he had been able to maintain his distance from his growing anger and so far had been able to control it. Secondly, he had also been able to dismiss all the slaves from his purpose apart from three who were different to all of the rest. He moved to the nearest sentry hut where he stood looking in through the open door at the sloppy soldiers who sat lazily drinking ale around a dirty card-spewed table.

These guards were the type of people who could not be employed anywhere else, and if they ever were to be then it certainly would not be for longer than a day - and they would not be employed at all if any other kind of replacement could be found. These were the worst of the worst. They were stupid, nasty misfits; they were mean, troublesome, corrupt, dirty, witless, grubby, cruel, dishonest, wicked, worthless, small-minded bullies, and they did not wash very often. Bill disliked them on sight (and secondly on smell). They did as little as possible and took great pleasure from having the slaves at their mercy.

These guards saw the slaves as nothing more than a way of making easy money; they did whatever was necessary to control them and to keep them as viable commodities so that their clients would want them - for so long as it gave them pleasure. Apart from this, they bullied and taunted them for many reasons, boredom being just one. They often used force instead of words and made full use of their power and position over these poor unfortunates. This made them feel better but led to very bad relationships between them and those who suffered at their hands. It also meant that other people, even those who needed them to keep the slaves healthy, the city residents and those who used them, all tried to keep as much distance between the guards and themselves as possible.

To be a slave guard was the lowest of the low. They had dirty fingernails, dirt between their toes and never washed their hands after going to the... well, you get the picture.

When the guards had given their latest bearded client enough of a wait to realise that they were in control, one of them got heavily to his feet and rearranged his heavy belt over his thick waist as he asked, "So, ya made up ya mind, have ya?"

The wizard slowly nodded his head up and down, as he in turn asked, "I want to talk to three of them. I have their numbers. Do you have somewhere we could go and talk - and that?"

Wiping his greasy lips with his sleeve, the guard smirked towards his comrades, "A wee talk is it? We have rooms and beds... and everything else you can think of. The cost goes up, mind - depending on as how long and what ya want to do with them. You pay for all damage done to them and to the room, understand?" Doing his best not to understand, Bill nodded.

"Right you are, tell me which ones then – and I'll find ya a nice place to talk to them, right?"

Soon Bill was sitting on a hard chair in a smelly room in a wooden hut where the bed had been removed at his request (and extra cost) to make his intent and conversation all the easier to proceed.

The door was kicked open and two guards came in dragging the first of the wizard's three chosen slaves. "Ya sure you don't want us to weaken 'em first... to make it easier for ya like... at a small cost?"

Shaking his hairy head, Bill replied that all he wanted to do was to talk, and that he was sure there would be no problems and that he definitely did *not* want them to weaken the poor chap as he looked weak enough already. With a reminder that any damage done to the prisoner or the room was on his back and any done to him was his own problem, the guards left him and the tall, thin, scared slave in relative peace.

"Won't you rest?" Bill asked his visitor, indicating an empty chair near the door. The slave studied the old man from under his eyelashes as he kept his head pointed to the ground and remained silent.

"Suit yourself. So, what do you want from life?"

Thinking this was yet another way to torture him, the slave kept quiet as the old man studied him.

After a short while, Bill continued by saying "So... you want to be like other people, find a wife and have a family with freedom to go where you want to go... I see... So it is anger and a desire for justice that keeps you going and why your energy is so high! Thank you, you can go now - and that."

Shaking his head, the prisoner backed to the door and banged on its worn panels until the two guards opened it. One grabbed the prisoner while the other guard gave Bill a sideways look as he remarked, "That was quick old un, are ya a sure that you huv finished with it? - it is still full payment if ya don't have the full time, you know." Nodding his understanding, Bill watched as the confused prisoner was taken away.

A short while later the door was pulled back and the guard asked if he was ready for the next of his choices. "Yes please," Bill said, forcing himself not to turn the guard into a slimy piece of plankton.

This interview was almost an exact repeat of the first, the difference being that this slave was female, and she snarled a lot more. Bill discovered that she wanted revenge and various ways to torture her tormentors. After that, she wanted to take up sewing napkins in a little shop she had once visited when she was on holiday with her parents when she was six years old. Smiling, Bill told her that she might just be able to have some of her desire in the near future, seeing as he was having problems with not interfering. She stood frowning at him until she was taken away.

The third was also female but she was much younger. She stood there more defiantly than the man but snarled less than the woman. She seemed to Bill to have more muscles than both of them put together. She had refused his offer of a seat and stood watching him with flaring nostrils. He sat stroking his bearded chin as he studied her from his chair thinking how wrong this whole city was. Finally, he asked her, "So, what do you want to do with your life - and that?"

She blinked a couple of times before replying in a dry voice that she would just love to own a palomino pony and to go riding through the hills of Vermeer with a picnic and some chilled wine. She did not really want to do any of these things of course, but she was a slave and was not happy so when she was asked what to her was a really stupid question, she replied with a stupider answer, just to keep the balance.

Wizard Bill explained to her that this was not the usual game of pretence or punishment that she was used to. Then he added that he really did want to know what she wanted from life.

Putting her head on one side, she studied the old man, wondering what he really wanted from her. She shrugged her shoulders and finally told him, "I don't wanna be a slave no more."

Waving his hand as if this had been agreed long ago, Bill repeated, "Yes, but what do you want to do with the rest of your life?"

Jutting her jaw in his direction and putting her hands on her hips, she said, "I want to be able to choose; to choose without having to be forced to do things. I want freedom and to not be bound by anything at all like getting money, or because society says I must, or because I am forced to by the guards. I want to be able to help people if I want - or not if I don't. I want to be me and to be free to do whatever I want, whenever I want to do it. Does that answer your question, Grandad?"

Smiling, the old man got to his feet and offered her his outstretched hand; she took it only after seeing that she was much younger and fitter than he was and could probably fight him to a standstill if she had to. This old man was tall and solid looking but she had often fought much younger and tougher-looking men so she felt safe if it came to blows. As she took his hand she waited for some trick to be pulled on her, she was ready not to be surprised by the latest torture, whatever form it would take.

Shaking her hand in a gentle but firm manner, he nodded as he told her, "Then we will see if you will still want what I can offer you once things here change as they are about to - and that. Normally of course, we do not interfere in things. But on this occasion I think I will make an exception and make a little difference to things - and that."

Letting go of her hand, he waved both of his in the air in front of him as he muttered words that had no meaning to the girl. When he stopped he was grinning as he said, "There... now it is up to them. I've put a small inhibitor spell on killing, but apart from that it's up to them to do what they want to do. It will eventually rebalance itself out as all things must, but those that take the chance could learn a great deal, and many will never have to come back. Now, are you ready?"

Taking a step away from him in case his madness was catching, she moved closer to the door. In the short time she had been held as a slave, she had been abused both mentally and physically, but the risk of madness and losing her awareness was the greatest threat and fear she had.

Nodding, Bill explained to her that this part of the world had changed and if she wanted to, she could go with him where she might be able to learn how to obtain her every wish if she still desired to do so. He told her that she was free to choose and that she could go with him or she could go wherever she wanted - for it was now up to her - as it was for the rest of the prisoners.

She pressed against the door and waited for his next move or crazy word.

"What has happened is that the prisoners and the guards have exchanged places," he explained. "Now it's up to the slaves to do what they will do. They can do anything to the guards except kill them for I can't have that. They can leave here and start new lives or they can return some of the gifts the guards had given them before they go. It is up to them. Now, have you made up your mind?"

"Where do you want to take me? I must go back soon," she told him, humouring him as she banged on the door, hoping the guards would come and get her so she could be rid of this strange old man and his stories that a part of her wanted to believe.

The door that should have been locked from the outside opened under the pressure of her banging. Turning, she ran out of the room and waited for the guards to surround her. When nothing happened, she moved over to the rail that looked down from the nearest prisoner viewing section to the slave pens below. As she looked down, she gasped in wonder at the sight that met her eyes.

Everything the old man had told her was true; slaves were throwing things down onto the guards who screamed in fear as they tried to hide from the missiles that dropped down into the pens around them. She looked further out over the city and saw masses of her fellow slaves making for its outskirts. She heard a voice at her side and turned to look at the wizard. "Who are you?" she asked, expecting to wake up any second to find this was just another one of her dreams.

Instead, she heard him tell her in a matter-of-fact voice, "I'm a wizard and I'm looking for someone who wants a life of study that will offer freedom. I want to offer you the chance to be that person - and that."

Thinking that her dreams were becoming ever the stranger, she told him, "Whatever you say, old man... let's go!"

Nodding, he waved his hands in a complicated pattern, and all at once they were not there anymore. Not that anyone noticed - what with the slaves either running away or punishing the guards. The rest of the citizens were hiding behind locked doors or packing their valuables and all of the visitors were leaving as fast as they could.

The city was never the same after this - neither were the guards, and especially neither was the girl.

# Chapter Five:
# Henry and Keryon

On a very cold, windy, and inhospitable plain in the eastern province of Teshnia, there stands a huge stone monastery where the renowned fighting monks live and train.

These are the famous fighting monks known throughout the whole region. No one is quite sure what these monks fight about, or how they started, but as they have the reputation of being experts in every kind of fighting style, no one has dared to ask them. The various warrior clans, soldiers, and people in the fighting professions all thought that they were much better fighters, but as none of them had yet found a good enough reason to fight any of the monks, this was still unproven. The few times anyone witnessed these monks fight was enough to seal their reputation as the best. They roamed the land doing whatever monks did when they were not fighting or practicing. Away from the monastery and wearing normal clothes, they looked just like anyone else; when they were in the monastery they wore bright, loose-fitting, different-coloured robes that swayed around them making impressive shushing sounds.

Every few years they would take in new disciples so that they would not get into a situation like the wizards had found themselves in - without having anyone to teach or impress. The life of the monks was thought to be a good one especially by those who had nothing. So, even though the odds on getting accepted were very low, it still looked better than starving, working, or begging, and so many came and many more were sent by their parents to seek entrance into the monastery. These hopefuls gathered outside on the wind-swept plain where they had to wait to be accepted or rejected.

This had become the ritual; they just sat and waited out in the cold wind while the monks inside the warm, snug monastery watched them. This process could take anything from a few hours to a week, or even longer, so the stories said. All of this time, they were being watched and judged from inside by the monks who would change the lives of the few who were accepted.

The monks would take only those they thought to be the right kind of humans. No one really knew what they thought the right kind of humans were, so boys of all ages and sizes were sent from all over the land by their poor parents to sit outside and wait. Those who came sat... and waited... until they were either called inside or sent home. More often than not, they became fed up and went away of their own accord.

This was the second day that the hopeful ones had sat watching the high walls in the expectation that they might be called inside. Already all of the older youths had been told to leave, and later some of the smaller children had been sent home. During the long night, a few others had slipped away under cover of darkness. Some of those left had started to play games or walk around until a figure appeared high up on the wall. They all turned to stare at it and its magnificent, fluttering clothes.

The figure pointed at a few of them telling them to go

away, as they were not wanted and would never become monks; the rest were to stay and wait. It became obvious that the ones who had been sent away were those that had been playing or moving around, and so the rest sat as still as possible as the first raindrop fell amongst them. At about the time the ninth raindrop hit the ground, a wizard named Henry appeared.

He glanced around him and nodded; noticing that the ground was beginning to get wet, he muttered a spell to keep himself dry from the increasing rain. He started to walk amongst the scattered young people who shivered as the wind and rain combined forces to get them as wet and cold as they could. As he searched among the seated children his spell kept him completely dry (even the undersides of his feet) so he was comfortable as he searched for someone with that right spirit and attitude.

Thinking he was another test, the young hopefuls tried to ignore him as he strolled amongst them, ready to answer his questions if and when he came to stand in front of them - which he did to a few of them. He asked questions such as, "You want what from life?"

"You... is that all?... your life."

"Now, how about you?... I see."

"Now what do you want? Good choice, young man."

"So then, how about you, youngster? What do you want to do with your life? Good luck to you then…."

"...you want... A what? Maybe you could achieve that, maybe not."

"Now what about you?"

He gave them little or no chance to answer his questions as he moved amongst them reading their energy. He continued to do this until he came to a stop in front of a small dark-skinned boy who was losing the fight to remain seated and stay unaffected from the now lashing rain and the puddle that was forming under him. The aspect of a small, dry man with mouse-coloured hair, beard, and moustache who was asking stupid questions that he was not even allowed to answer was the last straw.

Forgetting the warnings from his parents that this was his one and only chance, he also forgot the monks, he forgot his promises to his village, and even the one to himself; he forgot everything as he got to his feet and screamed at the surprised figure.

The wizard blinked down at him and smiled as he heard the boy scream at him.

"Who do you think you are? Making us act like some form of low animal. If that is what you want then go look in the forest. I have had enough! Sitting here all night and all day without a word - then you arrive and ask questions that you don't even let us answer! It is too much - I wouldn't treat an animal as badly and with so little respect. It is too much! - without respect there is nothing - so take your teachings and stuff them! I don't care anymore!"

He stood quivering with rage and from the cold, waiting to be sent home; he half expected to be dragged away, to be laughed at, or even hit for his insolence.

He expected many things to happen but what he did not expect was for the figure to clap his hands in obvious joy and then grin like a clown as he patted him on the shoulder, saying that he was the one. The boy watched him through half-closed eyes as the strange figure told him, "Splendid! Splendid! I agree with you - it is not a nice thing to do and I want no part of it. You are the one! So, if you do not want to be a performing animal, then what do you want to be?"

"I want to be treated as a person," the thin boy replied, unaware of the sidelong stares of the other drenched candidates.

Henry nodded in approval and folded his hands over his stomach at the answer, and then said that he could do that, especially as he did not know any other way of treating people. Extending the dry spell to include the boy, he explained that he was looking for someone with certain abilities and the right attitude who really wanted to learn to become a wizard, and that he thought he had found them. He added, "I can put you forward to the council who will give you the old once over and if they agree... and why would they not... then we will give you the chance to learn to become a wizard. If it's the kind of thing that you would like to consider? I could put you forward if you would like me to or I can leave you alone. It is really your choice."

Enjoying the freedom from the downpour and wanting to learn how they were being kept dry, the boy shook some of his soaking hair away from his face, and taking a last look around, looked deep into the old man's dark eyes, telling him, "I would like this chance you say you are offering. I cannot stay here, whatever happens. If I go home, my parents and village will be disappointed and still not have enough food for me. Now that the monks won't have me there is nothing left for me - so I will not miss this chance you offer." He sighed heavily and shook his wet head again as he said, "If this is a test, then I did what I did, and will live with what I did. I would like to go with you, please, and be given the chance to learn - as long as I am treated as a person - or left alone to make my own way from there."

Nodding and smiling, Henry replied, "Very good... now, shall we walk to over there a-ways?" They moved away from the other hopeful candidates. "Good, this will do just fine." Then, as an afterthought, the old man added, "My name is Henry Darkmoore, Darkmoore with an e, and I am a wizard with a wiz."

When the boy did not react to his attempted joke, as he was too wet, tired, and scared to do so, Henry shook his head as they moved even further away from the rest of the candidates. The rain was now cutting visibility down to a few yards, so when they vanished the other candidates were not surprised that the two figures faded from view.

# Chapter Six: Joe and Myrtle

A large wooden barn stood in the middle of a grassy field. The farm to which it belonged had the usual amount of barns set closer to the farmhouse, so this building was unusual - not just for its size - but also for it being extra. It was painted a bright white colour both outside and in. This also was not the way that things were normally done, but then this barn had been built for holding celebrations and the white interior helped keep it bright and stopped it from being mistaken for an ordinary barn.

It could still be used if the other barns became damp, or full of something such as relatives (who come to stay when the house was full of lambs), or worts or especially if one of the other barns happened to fall down. This particular barn could go months in the winter without seeing a human being and a good few weeks in the summer, but when it did, it saw a large amount of them. Today it was going to be the scene of more human activity than it had ever seen before - as today was the farmers' first local celebration of Cow Day (or The Day of the Cow).

Some time ago these farmers had noticed that there were not as many parties and get-ye-togethers as they would have liked. They had a meeting to discuss the matter and during it someone suggested that they should rejoice in their animals by holding a special day for celebrating them. All agreed, for it was only at meetings that they had a chance to gossip, drink, eat, dance, complain, exchange views, and find employment or employees. It was also the only time when the young farmers could meet prospective partners, so the idea was readily accepted by one and all.

Today it was the Cows's turn, where the farmers would give thanks for all the milk, leather, calves, and cheese - as well as giving them this excuse to celebrate. This was to be the largest and greatest celebration so far and the first to honour the magnificent cow.[5]As the owners (and those who lived near enough to be called on to help) were busy - preparing food and carrying it into the hall, putting up decorations, sweeping the floor, and generally preparing to boogie - a figure of an old man with a long beard was briefly seen on the East side of the Barn.

He looked around - muttered something like, "Damn! 'Tis too early - I should have known it![6]" - then he moved to the corner and disappeared before anyone could stop him. This gave the workers a subject to talk about for most of the afternoon as they tried to understand the meaning of such a vision, and then embellishing the story in preparation to tell the rest of the Cow Day celebrants when they arrived.

Later that evening, the wagons and the animals that pulled them rested in front of the barn or in the nearby fields while their owners changed into their good clothes (some even put on shoes instead of their usual boots or bare feet). Soon the place filled with dancing couples moving to the

---

[5] There were, of course, no cows invited. This may seem mean but, as part of the celebration was to praise the many various parts of the cow that were used by the farmers, perhaps it was a good thing after all.

[6] Joe did not have any problem with starting to talk again - as he had never stopped. He talked to himself quite a lot and often went into one of the towns where talking was the norm.

sound of the music makers. This consisted of a man with a homemade snare drum, a violinist, a flute player, another violinist, a guitar that often needed to be tuned, an aging piano, and something that looked like it had been made from skin, bones, and branches, and which sounded the way it looked. The music was loud and played enthusiastically as the musicians were "wetted good and proper."

All of this said that Cow Day was going to be a great success, and if the amount of food, drink, and anticipation that now filled the great space were anything to go by then Cow Day was sure to become a regular feature. As the day turned into night, there became almost as much activity around the barn as there was within it, only with less light. This consisted of farmers swapping drinks and stories, people coming or going to check on the animals, to answer the call of nature, to catch up on gossip, or even to fight over some small matter. A small number of them left for a quick sleep - while others just left the barn to get some fresh air. These activities increased with the volume of drink taken and the rise in temperature inside the barn.

Most of the people outside had their minds on what they were doing but in spite of this one man did notice the wizard named Joe, who was standing next to the largest and only tree in the next field. He looked very jolly which was part of the reason why he was not, in fact, jolly - the expectation was too high for him to keep up.

As the wizard blinked at the light that poured from the open doors of the building, he muttered to himself, "This is better, Joe boy, bit close to the damn tree though... I hate this stuff. Now, where are all the young ones?"

The person who had seen him shouted out to let

everyone know that the vision was back. The vision strode towards the barn, and then stopped half a field away in front of it, squinting until his eyes were only mere slits. He moved his head up and down, then to the left and then to the right.

As the farmers and their families poured out of the barn and stood looking at him he said, "Don't tell me I have come all this way for nothing? There must be something, Joe. Look harder, boy!" he told himself harshly.

The crowd of cow celebrants stood pointing at the old man who folded his arms over his thin chest and waited. Soon he was facing sixty-nine curious, drunk, near drunk, past drunk, sober, past sober, frightened, angry, curious, half asleep, half awake, fascinated and (in a couple of cases) bored farmers. They formed rows of half-horseshoe patterns in front of him, and then stood waiting for someone else to act first. Once someone did or said something then they would each be more than ready to give advice on a better way of doing it or to criticise it in two directions, but until someone else made the first move they were content to wait.

Still frowning at the glare that came from the open doors of the barn, the Wizard scanned the entire party. I say the entire party but this was not strictly true, for some were not there watching the sight of an old wizard talking to himself.

Kenny was drunker than a beer barrel and was sleeping in his wagon; ma Tell was looking for mad Mary and silly Billy who were in the process of looking for physical similarities between themselves and their farm animals and so were not noticing anything else; Marty was also sleeping only underneath his wagon. Then there was Doug the mender, who was sleeping and dreaming of strange visions and so missed very little as his dreams were so much more fulfilling than an old skinny man with a long beard who talked to himself. There were also three couples, engaged in hugging and kissing behind the barn and so did not care about anything else.

The wizard named Joe had already checked them all out and had found that their energy was lacking in everything but curiosity and that they were all madder than even wizard Francis who wrote in books. Joe pointed to a tall yellow-haired girl of indeterminate age and beckoned to her with his index finger.

Amongst half warnings from her family and neighbours, she stumbled forward in spite of herself until she was facing him and looking down into his dark eyes. "What do you want from this life?" he asked with his hands on his hips. Then, without waiting for an answer, he read the energy that was pouring from her every limb. Nodding and smiling he said, "You'll do." Then they disappeared, leaving the farmers with enough to talk and speculate about to last for the next few years.

The parents of the girl were secretly happy that she had gone, as she was of marrying age and no one had shown any interest in making her their wife; besides, she ate enough for three while only doing the work of two; and anyway they wanted to use her room for the winter sacks of spuds and worts. She would need feeding while taking up room but now that she was gone they would be famous. They knew that she had not been that happy with her life and now she had given them more than they had ever dared hope for - fame. The attendees of the Cow Day celebration searched for her for an hour or so before getting on with the party - after all, it was the first Cow Day ever.

# Chapter Seven: Reginald and Mountain Boy

The boy had been climbing the mountain for a few days now and the mountain still did not care, nor had it even noticed. He had started many miles below where the masses of rocks were nothing but a gentle slope. Soon it had become steeper with every foot that he climbed until it was almost vertical. Many mountains are like that; some are mostly slopes at different angles, some even lean inwards before going more outwards and then upwards again. Mountains also come in many different colours as well (I like the grey ones myself).

The boy had come seeking enlightenment, believing that the age of the mountain and its contained wisdom would somehow rub off on him or, better still, that he would meet the spirit of the mountain who would receive his sacrifice. All that had rubbed off on him so far however, was rock dust, dirt, some form of weed, dew, and a very old bird's nest complete with ancient eggs. He had nowhere else to go, for he had abandoned his old life just as it was getting ready to abandon him, and so he kept climbing.

Now he would dedicate his life to seeking knowledge. Who better to learn from than one of the oldest and biggest things in the land: the mountain. And if it rejected him then so be it. Since making this promise to himself, he had spent a lot of time getting dirtier and collecting more bruises and scratches as he crawled slowly up the huge grey mass that towered ever above him.

The last few days he had lost the gnawing pain of hunger. He was able to quench his thirst from the morning dew or from the mist when it covered everything, including his clothes. This provided him with just enough liquid to enable him to keep climbing. All of his thoughts now centred on just one thing - getting to the top - no matter what it took (well, either that or until the God of the mountain accepted the humble sacrifice of his life).

He had lost most of his mind due to hunger and desperation and as there had not been a lot to lose in the first place, it had been easy enough to lose the rest. He clung on to the mountain and to the one thing that still made any sense to him, to get to the top and/or meet the mountain God. This was where he would either be accepted, sacrificed by it, given knowledge, or killed for his insolence.

He was as filthy as only someone who had been climbing a dirty mountain with clothes that were none too clean to start with, who had been sleeping on, hanging from, exposed to all weathers and breathing in a mountain, could be. His hands and knees bled, scratched raw under their layer of filth and his hair stood out as if it was trying to escape from his head. His eyes were wild things seeking and seeing only the next handhold, and he smelt more of the mountain than himself.

Many times he had nearly fallen to his death only to save himself at the last moment by luck more often than by skill. Now, though he did not know it, his target was finally within his reach. Just a few more yards above him, and he would be at his final destination, for even mountains do not go on forever, they just seem to. Making his tormented, bleeding right hand grab yet another outcropping, he gritted his teeth against the pain, concentrating only on the patch of rock just above his face, and, in this way, gained another few feet of height.

On reaching the summit he did not even realise that he had finally reached his goal. He gasped and rolled onto his back and lay panting noisily, thinking that it was just another wide ledge. After a while, he was finally able to open his eyes. He saw nothing but sky above him and quite a lot around him as well. Slowly he realised that there was mountain nowhere but under him and that he really had made it. Still panting from his efforts, he raised his aching body up on his elbows and gave a silent prayer of gratitude to the mountain God.

As he prayed he heard someone say in a very polite voice, "Errm... er, sorry to disturb you old chap, but can I... er... ask you a question? Or do I come back a little later when you have recovered a bit more?"

With tears in his eyes, the boy whispered that anything the Great God of the Mountain wanted to do with him was all right with him, including, and especially, ending his miserable and meaningless life.

There was a pause as the wizard tried to work out what the boy was saying.

"Oh... no, I am not a God, and... er... nor do I want your life - as I still have some of my own left, but... um... thanks for the offer - it was extremely kind of you... hmm, yes it was."

The youth rolled onto his back so he could see where the sound was coming from. He saw a vision of an old fat man in a grey garb the colour of the mountain (well, the colour of

this mountain at this particular time anyway) reclining on a rock. The bedraggled youth instantly rolled back onto his front and thrust his face into the ground. In his mind, he went over the brief image he had seen above him. It had been a vision of a plump, light brown bearded man who lay reclined against a small rock, dressed in a rock-coloured garment that covered him from his neck down, complete with hood. The boy banged his face into the mountain in thanks for being blessed with seeing the God of the mountain.

At the sound of the contact that the young man's head made against the rocks, the wizard (whose name was Reginald) asked him, "Doesn't that... er... hurt?"

The muffled reply went something like, "Muffin is too mufti hoof a sacrifice jut to be free is enough. Flease tell me wharf you will if me."

Shaking his head Reginald asked him, "Look, old boy, would you... er... mind awfully taking your head away from the... um... dirt as it makes it terribly difficult to understand what you are... um... saying."

The trembling boy raised his face from the gravel that had not stuck to him and stared towards the vision with closed eyes.

"Thank you my boy, now hmm, could I possibly ask you a question?"

The boy nodded vigorously. Then through bruised lips he revealed, "I am the son of a Fletcher and am yours to do with as is your will. O Great Mountain Spirit, I would willingly give thee my soul if only it was worthy of sacrifice."

The old man waved his hand in dismissal, saying, "I do

not think that will be... er... um... necessary, especially since I am not a spirit or a God or... er... anything special. I am just someone who umm, has spent his life, well a lot of it anyway... hmm... you could say most of it really... Um... up to this time at least. Now where was I? O yes... studying certain... er... subjects rather than... um... others. My name is Reginald by the way and I... er... am a wizard. Have I said that already? Would you like an apple they are... er... um... rather good?"

The youth moved his bleeding and bruised body until he was finally kneeling in front of the old man. Then, half sitting and half bowing, he gave the wizard a superior smile saying, "You are testing me. I am not worthy, and I know that I come from a long line of unbelievers. Nay! I will do what I can, but I fear I am not good enough for thee to even consider wasting thy golden words on... I am yours." With the last words, he again threw himself face down on the ground.

The seconds ticked by and when no reply came, the boy began to wonder if the God had taken him at his words and had gone away. Risking a glance in the general direction of where the figure had been, he saw that it had not moved except to scratch its nose.

On seeing the boy's glance, the wizard asked, "Would you like a drink or... um... something to eat? I am a little peckish myself so it... er... would be no trouble." Suddenly there appeared food and drink on a pure white cloth spread out on a small table between them. The youth forgot in whose presence he thought himself to be, and grabbed a cool bottle of water and drank deeply.

"Er... If I were you, I would not drink too much too soon

as the umm... shock to the body could cause... er... severe effects, even that of dying I have heard. Now, what... um... shall I have first?"

The boy dropped the bottle and gaped at the old man who reached for a dainty cake and nibbled at its icing.

Much later… after the boy had eaten and drunk enough to regain at least some of his senses[7]… anyway, much later he sat talking to the wizard as if they were old friends from way back when... whenever that had been, if it had, which it had not... but you get the idea... or I hope you do anyway.

The old man found that the boy's normal speech was as flowery as a greenhouse that was full of manure and extremely fine seeds. He was saying, "Thee are indeed great to share thou sparse food with one who is not worthy to clean your feet. I will never be worthy to rise above a cockroach. This is yet another sign indicating your greatness and I will go from one end of the world to the other upholding thy reputation to all and sundry, even though I be tortured to say otherwise. For only in so doing could I ever start to repay the honour that thou has paid to one who is totally ungrateful even to be breathing the same air as one as pure as thy great self. It would be a pleasure to undertake torture if only thou will accept such a pitiful gift of my loyalty and dedication to you. I am but a bit of dirt that thou may mould or throw, but if it pleases you, great one, could one as poor and insignificant as me ask you a question?"

Reginald, who had been wondering if he had room for

---

[7] Well, nearly as many as he had had before he had started on this adventure - which were not that many - for he had never had the time to really give them the chance to grow as he had been quite busy reading books about knights and such like.

the last éclair, glanced at him and mumbled his consent as he reached for the cake.

"I know that I have no right and, and my only reason for asking is so that I might gain knowledge and save myself a good deal of hard work that I may see my ungrateful life for just how worthless it really has been. I know that I should not really... I really should not ask... for the act of truth seeking is to be able to give without hope. I think therefore that I should take the hardest route if I am worthy of even that great task, no matter what the risk."

Through a mouthful of creamy éclair, the wizard told him. "Err, could you... um... just get on with it, please."

Bowing as well as he could from his sitting position, the youth asked, "How did you arrive at this point and time, I mean no disrespect - but why did you take on the form of an old man? One such as you could appear in any form, size and shape, so therefore I wondered." He did not say that he thought the aspect of an old man with a large belly and greasy hair, not to mention the large red nose and piggy eyes, was not that favourable in comparison to the huge and magnificent mountain. He also did not say that he found the habit of throwing in "er"s and "umm"s into sentences very annoying.

The old man interrupted his thoughts while wiping cream from his beard and moustache by asking him, "Now, um... ah, I know what I wanted to ask you. What do you... er... want from life? I mean more... um... than anything else, really... ah... want?"

The boy bowed his head as his thoughts whirled, knowing that only the absolute and total truth was good enough for one as wise as this particular old man, spirit, or mountain god. After some while he finally replied, "I would like to become worthy to ascend to the height where I could become a seeker of knowledge, and... and..."

Reginald waved his hand and the boy stopped in mid-sentence. He had not meant to, but suddenly the boy lost the ability to speak, think, or even move. This was thanks to a small spell (called a stilling spell) that all young wizards use on each other until they learn how to counteract it. Nodding in appreciation at the silence, the man asked, "Now, dear boy, do you care what... er... you seek?" He looked at the figure then told it, "I see... hmm, another question if I... er, may? Now look - you... um... have me doing it, huh! I mean no disrespect but do you... umm, really have to talk like that? It is a trifle irritating old chap if you... er... um... see what I mean? O, sorry... er... I see that as far as you are umm, concerned... you do have to talk like that. Well, what a sorry state you are in. I see that with food and rest, your body will recover; but your mind is very confused, although at the same time, you do seem to have the right spirit. Oh well, here goes."

Snapping his fingers, the old man smiled across at the figure that, on finding his voice had returned, replied, "I knew thou were one of the wisest and most powerful of all of the spirits. Thank you for giving me the time to witness thy power firsthand. I wish to seek truth and justice and to be able to at least ask the answer to the ultimate question."

Sighing, the old man told him that he was seeking people who were looking to learn how to seek knowledge. The boy prostrated himself yet again, so Reginald then asked him if he was ready and, not waiting for an answer, allowed the spell of silence to cover the boy once again. Sighing heavily the wizard shrugged his shoulders before moving his hands, making the remaining food, tablecloth, and table all disappear; three seconds later, he and the boy vanished, leaving only a few crumbs on the empty, quiet mountain.

# Chapter Eight: Albert and Mocker

The south-western lands are covered almost entirely by various kinds of forests that encompass such a vast distance that different parts of it have different names. It is so extensive that it has different seasons, for just one cannot cover it all. There are stories that entire cities live inside it. Cities not yet found by anyone else in the world; and so the residents of these hidden cities thought that they were the only people on the planet. Many of the known cities were unknown unless you knew where to look for them or came upon them by mistake. There was also a story that these forests were so vast that there was a sea in the middle of them, but no one knew about that either.

In a very minute part of this continental forest a wizard appeared. He became visible very slowly, for he was tired and a little grumpy after his last few attempts at finding anyone who (even after a little bit of training) could be considered as apprentice material, and failing. As he walked along the path, he grumbled as he normally did, this time to the trees and bushes, as if it was somehow their fault. His name was Albert although at school his nickname was Greens, for his father owned a greengrocer's shop and when he was young he'd had nightmares of becoming a potato. He had neatly trimmed brown hair, beard, and moustache that were slowly going grey, and he often enjoyed a pint or three of beer.

He became so intent on his grumbling and complaining that he did not notice a group of small faces that crouched watching him from behind some of the thick underbrush. These faces belonged to the children who were all members of the True Fellowship of the Forest (or T.F.O.T.F.s as they called themselves). They saw very few other humans outside their Fellowship, and as they considered themselves a race apart and therefore superior, those they did meet were treated with disdain at best and death at worst. The T.F.O.T.F.s knew they were the best and that everyone else was less important than they were, so any visitor who came near was offered sharp arrows at the first meeting - and then things would often get worse. Due to this, the few other forest dwellers that knew of their existence left them alone.

The faces that watched the complaining wizard were children of the T.F.O.T.F.'s. Their arrows were not quite as sharp as their elders were, nor were they as suspicious as their parents. They were a lot more curious, and in spite of the many stories told of non-T.F.O.T.F.s eating children, they still watched the old man to see what he would do as he walked along grumbling loudly to himself. They moved quietly through the undergrowth to where they could watch him while still keeping the option to run away if the need arose. When it did, they all crept slowly and quietly backwards out of sight - all that is except for one, who did not hear the whispered cautious words telling them to move away. Instead, he remained crouched beside a bush studying the strange clothes and behaviour of the wizard until the wizard finally became aware of him.

"Oh dear! I must be getting old or something... I nearly missed you, young good sir. Good day to you... and who might you be on such a fine day?"

The eyes of the child widened in terror as it tried to back into the restricting bush that had begun to hold him fast.

"I mean you no harm, young sir. Look, I will move away... nothing in my hands... see? I am just on a walk to see what I can see and... Hmm, so there are more of you, are there?" He glanced at where the rest of the young band hid further away behind solid trees, and he was just about to repeat his words when an idea came to him. "Now young sir, why are you still here? I see that you have freed yourself from that bothersome bush. Are you especially brave? Not particularly stupid, no! Bright brained? Again... not especially. So then, what keeps you so close? And why do you study my face so intently as if trying to read my whole character from it? Speak up, young 'un!"

The child put its head on one side then made a sort of animal noise that was somewhere between a groan and a squeak. Creaking noises came from his knee joints as the old man crouched down until his face was on a level with that of the child's. From this precarious balancing position, he spoke to the child in slow-worded phrases, "I am a friend. I will not harm you. I am really stupid for I see that you do not understand me, do you?"

The boy smiled and nodded his head as he gasped out one word, "Mocker," then put his finger to his chest.

Scratching his beard the wizard became aware that the other children had now run away to find their parents. Pointing to his own chest he said, "My name is Albert, how do you do?" Holding out his hand, it hovered in between them for a few seconds, then slowly the boy put his own briefly into it and then tucked it away again as if it were a treasured possession (as indeed it was).

The brief contact had been enough to the now wide-awake wizard[8] to inform him of the child's history and the reason why he had not answered him. At the same time, he also became aware of all the grownup T.F.O.T.F.'s who were now pounding towards them. Getting stiffly to his feet, he mouthed to the child, "So, young 'un, you are deaf then? Not a good thing when your kind puts so much pressure onto hearing all of the forest and its ways. You are bright, you are unhappy, and your grownups are coming. What do you want from life? O yes, please allow me to touch you." Again he offered his hand to the boy, who touched his leathery palm with his fingers as if it were a fish that any minute would flick away leaving him with just a few drops of water on his face.

The wizard was saying, "So your present life is not so good? You feel different and everyone else treated you as the least important member of your group. Good, so you would like the chance then to change it? Right, here we go then. Better, hurry before I have to do something to the silly grownups that are getting ready to attack me... Here lad, grab my hand."

With that, they were completely gone. They were so gone in fact, that in spite of the fine forest skills of even the best T.F.O.T.F. trackers, no sign of them was ever found. They never were able to find out how an old man carrying a young child was able to move out of their range without leaving a single sign. They thought that it must be magic - which, of course, it was.

---

[8] Albert was the only wizard who had to touch things to obtain information from them, while most of the others could do this from a distance.

# Chapter Nine: Martin and Follia

To say it was a castle was to say that the sky went on a bit. It was as if someone had taken a castle factory full of castles then added a few large cities and a small mountain or two of dirt along with lots of grassy squares with handfuls of odd trees on them. Then they had squashed the whole lot together until it became one huge, ugly, and enormous castle-city-village-cum-industrial-complex thing. It was very long, very deep, very, very high, and even longer than both of the other two put together. As they were still constantly building and replacing chunks of it, no one really knew how it would end up.

There were many levels starting at the deepest cells, used mainly as wine cellars, up to the highest turrets, where the soldiers patrolled and the birds nested. More than a mountain of rock and five forests had gone into its structure. It was huge, bigger than extensive, gigantic, immense, colossal, tremendous, mammoth, enormous, vast, and as it was massively abundant and... and... well you get the idea?

In the middle of the night, high on one of the many walkways where the soldiers kept watch, a wizard appeared. He was tall and thickset with faded dark hair and a beard that he shook along with his head as he adjusted his clothes, that is, he turned them into warmer clothes to help him to adjust to the change in climate. Then he wiped his moustache with the back of his hand, spelled a cigar, and puffed on it a few times before he was ready to look around. He turned to where the nearest form of life existed (he ignored the birds sleeping in their nests, the mice that ran along the inside of the walls, the plants and ferns that grew on the outside of the wall, and the millions of various insect life that lived everywhere else) and started to walk towards it.

Turning a corner, he found a soldier draped against his spear with a half-smile on his lips. The wizard, named Martin, strolled towards the dozing soldier who came half-awake and, shifting his weight, adjusted his spear and asked who went there in a voice that didn't really care one way or the other.

He reasoned that who but a friend could get, or would want to get, this high – besides, he was having a dream about fried toast and Megan and wanted to get back to them before the toast, or Megan, began to cool. Frowning, he asked out of habit, "Friend, or foe?"

Martin stopped in front of the soldier who was just beginning to realise that he was not facing his sergeant, another soldier, or even a lost citizen. He tried to move his spear and point it at the intruder. Long before his limbs had obeyed his sleepy commands the wizard had waved his hand in front of the soldier's face as he replied, "Actually, I am neither, but let's not worry about that, shall we? I want to ask you some questions and you are going to answer them for me. Do you understand?"

"I want to answer questions," the dazed man replied, his voice even sleepier as he dropped his spear that fell (accompanied by a loud rattling noise) onto the ground - but only after first hitting his foot and making him give a little shout.

"Shh! Be quiet, man!" Martin told him, looking around.

"Quiet," repeated the soldier dreamily.

Ignoring the reply, Martin asked him, "How many people live in this castle city altogether?"

"Nobody knows for sure," the sleeping soldier replied. Nodding his head, the wizard folded his arms, keeping his right hand free to hold the cigar and to stroke his moustache to aid his thinking as he produced another spell. Soon he blinked the spell away and nodded slowly, "I didn't know that there were that many people anywhere - let alone all in one place - truly amazing! So many people all living near one another and all of the time as well. They must really like each other is all I can say." He looked at the guard who stared into space not seeing anything and only hearing Martin's voice when he made it into his commanding voice. When he mumbled or talked normally, the soldier heard nothing. "Now my man, please can you tell me, who lives where?" (Commanding voice, you see.)

The sleeping soldier replied, "Overlords live in the highest points under the roof, as they are the biggest rooms with the best views. Their families and courtesans live near or on the next level under them. The servers live nearby in smaller shared rooms, then the cooks and laundries, then the merchants and trades-people, then the soldiers who live underneath them at the perimeter, then the other servers live outside, as do the lower trades-people, and then the city folk live in the surroundings and everywhere else...."

"Thank you... now, where do the children live? Do they have a place where only they go?"

"Children live with their parents, or with those they serve, they go where they are sent and--"

Suddenly a blue flash blinded them both as it broke the spell on the soldier, who looked the old man up and down, "Who are you?" he asked in a surprised and slightly angry voice as he felt for his spear in the darkness.

With his full attention on the apparition that had just appeared, Martin clicked his fingers and the soldier went back to sleep missing the next question completely, as Martin asked the new arrival, "Who are you?"

Now that the smoke had thinned, he could make out the form of a tall man in a flowing, dark blue robe with many designs picked out in yellow and gold woven into it. The man wearing these garments looked even taller because of his tall pointed hat that also had some patterns around it. The apparition folded his arms across his chest before replying in a deep imposing voice, "I am the Magician who protects the ruling families and all those who serve them. Therefore, this entire castle city comes under my protection. Now, who are you? And what do you want?"

Martin smiled his best wizard smile as he said, "Nice voice effect by the way. So you detected some magic going on and flew here to protect your charges and your area? You really are up to the job, my compliments to you."

The other old man nodded, accepting the compliment then frowned, indicating that his question was still pending. It soon was.

"I am wizard Martin, trained by Theodore the fourth and abiding in the area of Pearland. Would you like a cigar?"

Stroking his long grey-blue beard the magician shook his head at the offer of a cigar "A wizard, huh? I thought you had all perished a long time ago. It is good to know there are still a few left who know the old ways. I am Algernon

Malkerith," he revealed, giving a small bow.

The wizard stroked his own beard and gave back the bow before he could crease it, confessing, "We thought all of you magicians had long gone, too. It's nice to see that we were wrong. Greetings to you, brother magic-wielder! There are still a few of us wizards left in odd places, thank you."

They stood watching each other as if trying to remember every detail of the other - which in actual fact was exactly what they were doing - for part of protecting yourself is knowing as much as possible about anyone who could cause you trouble (say, if they distort their form or something). This was necessary, as was knowing as much about yourself (especially your identity) as you could, for it could save your life. The more you could know about the person you were fighting, as in exactly how they looked and felt, the more they could not fool you by images when you were fighting for power, say. It is also wise to find and remember the size and type of the other one's spells. To do this, other spells were used to aid memory so if they had to hurl spells at each other, then at least they would start on equal terms.

The wizard revealed, "I am here to see if I can find anyone who is capable of learning our wisdom. In short, we need apprentices and vessels to pass on our knowledge to before we all move on. I thought this would be as good place as any, since there are so many people who abide here. I didn't know this city was protected or I would have asked permission first. I do not mean to intrude and so I will take my leave and leave."

The soldier took this moment to groan in his sleep and both men waved another sleeping spell at him at the same time. Realising that they both had done exactly the same thing, they laughed aloud at the poor sleeping soldier. "Perhaps one of us should take away their spell, otherwise he will sleep for days?" Martin suggested, turning his head slightly to one side as he added, "I'll take away mine, after all, it is your domain and I would not want to interfere in any way."

Algernon gave him a small bow that clashed with his costume but went well with his shoes, and said, "Can I suggest that we both take our spells away with us so that we can adjourn to my apartments?"

Martin nodded and relaxed as Algernon waved his hand in front of them, and instead of the windy cold walkway, a room with a large table set with food appeared to one side. Nodding his acceptance, Martin stepped forward, followed by the magician. They took their spells with them as they entered into the Magician's room that was actually three miles away from the windy, turreted walkway.

The soldier woke up just as the last trace of the entrance to the room disappeared, leaving behind a disgruntled walkway (or as disgruntled as a walkway can get). The soldier checked his body from the inside to make sure that it was all there. Then, dismissing the dream about men in funny clothes, he tried instead to keep the image of a hot Megan in his mind. As he bent to retrieve his spear, he told himself, "I'd better stay awake - or I'll never get upgraded and will have to spend the rest of my life guarding this boring area of stone where nothing ever happens."

The two wielders of magic sat eating from a meal that never got cold or even got to the stage where it begins to look as if you should not be eating it, and as they ate they talked. "This is a fine place you have here, it must be good work, looking after a province?" Martin said.

Helping himself to another drink of wine, Algernon replied, "It can be boring - but on the whole it is easy work and I do get a lot of time to myself for research." Putting down his glass, Martin reached forward to help himself to some bread and cheese as the magician asked, "So, you are looking for an apprentice?"

Martin swallowed the last of his chicken. "We are all going to die one day, and without people to take on our role, our work becomes something less than meaningless," he replied. "Or so it has begun to look to us," he added, in case the magician did not agree with him. Placing a piece of pâté-laden bread into his mouth, Algernon nodded as he chewed, then once he was capable of talking he confided, "I have an apprentice... well, two really... you cannot have them, but help yourself to anyone else in the city who might want to become your apprentice. No one comes to mind, though, but please feel free to see what you can find."

They finished their meal in silence except for the smacking of lips and occasional sighs of appreciation, then Martin thanked him for his generosity. Algernon bowed, blinked away the food and stepped back, leaving the whole floor free for Martin. Standing to his full height, Martin half closed his eyes and slowly twirled around in a circle with his left hand extended out in front of him, fingers splayed. He finally came to a stop where he had started. Opening his eyes, he told Algernon, "I see what you mean!" He pointed to a place on the wall that looked exactly like any other, "How about them?"

"You really must be desperate! I mean no disrespect to you, but would you really take on a child like that from a no family group?" Before Martin could answer he continued, "Well, it's your choice and no business of mine - so please, be my guest." They stood and bowed to each other and Martin was just able to dodge the top of the pointed hat as it came towards his left eye.

Seconds later, Martin was standing at the doorway of a long, wide, and crowded room where many children filled the many cots lining both sides of the walls. He drifted between them until he came to one where a very small and very, very round child slept unsoundly. She had bright red hair and spots all over her face. Looking down at her, he said to the sluggish air, "This is the one - she is seen as a total misfit, and treated accordingly. To them she is the lowest of the low, a child with no parents and no prospects, and she never will have any if she stays here. The other children bully her while the people who are in charge of the children ignore her. She is so very unhappy and desperate for anything other than what she now has.

"Come, my little one, tell me your desires."

The child stirred in her sleep, then sat up and rubbed her eyes. In a sleepy voice that was no more than a whisper, she said, "Want special, not hurt me."

Rubbing his hands, Martin told her, "I can take you to a place where you may get the chance to become just that. Would you like the chance of a new life?"

Now very awake, the child crawled along the bed to its end. She got up on her knees and held out her arms to him saying, "Please... yes... very mucher... ta."

Folding his arms around her, Martin helped her off the bed and onto the floor. Then, gripping her hand as tightly as he dared, he said a few words to the sleepy air and then they were gone. Which left the other children with no one to tease or compare themselves with when they woke up the next morning. And on top of this, they were forced by the adults to spend hours searching all over the castle for her.

# Chapter Ten: The Council Meets

As I said before, Pearland is a place of no distinctive value - geographical, animal, or vegetable - and it leads to nowhere in particular (although there are better and shorter ways of getting there). It is of interest to neither man nor beast and, because of all of the above, it is ideal for wizards.

In a part of this featureless, wind-swept place, a chair suddenly appeared, floating in the air a few feet from the ground. It was an old wooden framed chair with a brown indented leather seat, worn cushioned arms, and a back that had seen much use in its many years of existence. Slowly the chair floated down to the ground until it settled on its four feet.

Then the skinny wizened wrinkled form of wizard Arnold materialized, floating in the air just above the seat. He glanced around and then down at the chair before he cautiously floated down into and onto it until he came to rest, fitting its worn, intricately-shaped depths exactly. He was holding a long staff across his knees and he again looked quickly around. Peering into the endless, flat, featureless landscape, he told himself, the chair, and his personal staff in still a surprisingly loud and deep voice, "So I am the first, am I? Very good! Now I have time to get comfortable before anyone else gets here." He squirmed into an even more comfortable position and in seconds was fast asleep.

The wind blew across the hard ground and rattled the nine bushes and the one solitary tree that somehow managed to survive in the rocky, dry ground. As the wind approached the sleeping much-wrinkled figure, it slowed down, then crept slowly past until it was well away from the wizard. It only then picked up speed and went on its windy way, smiling to itself as only the wind can.

Much later, another chair appeared close to the snoring Arnold. This one was taller, thicker, and much, much wider. It was made from the largest, strongest pieces of everything that it was made from, and even then had been reinforced all over again.

Its leather had once been a deep wine red when it was new, but now it had become a sickly brown cracking constipation colour. It was not only taller, wider and more reinforced but it was also more ornate than Arnold's chair. The arms were carved into a leafy pattern that extended up the back where, at the top and in the middle of the backrest, it had a small indentation where once there had been a crest, while the thick legs ended in small serpent feet covering brass wheels. It even had a rack along one side for its owner's staff to sit in.

This wonderful object had cost a small fortune when purchased many, many years before, and it had been the envy of many. Now it smelt of old meals, sour milk, pipe tobacco, soap, new and used leather, and even older men, mixed with horsehair and a few dead insects. It smelt, in fact, quite a lot like its owner - and was now the envy of no one. Floating just above its faded, squashed, reinforced surface appeared Roger: the largest, fattest, and roundest wizard of them all. He looked down at his sleeping friend and allowed himself a huge grin as he slowly floated down and down until he made full bodily contact with his ornate smelly chair. When they were once again one, he coughed loudly to wake his friend before he became too bored with his own company.

Opening his eyes, the older, smaller man nodded at him, gave a small stretch using just his arms and back, and commented happily, "I was first!"

The larger wizard looked around at the empty landscape as he replied, "Arnold... you are always the first to arrive."

"Well I am... that's all!" From under his wrinkled lids, Arnold glanced up at his friend, saying, "I see that your voice has come back?"

Shaking his head and smiling, the larger man remarked, "I have been practicing. Besides, surely, you mean that you can hear rather than see that my voice has improved, nay come back." Arnold wrinkled his nose and closed his eyes as Roger confessed, "It would seem that going back to using words will mean that we will have to put up with each other's strange little ways."

His companion (who was first) asked, "What exactly do you mean by 'strange little ways' may I ask?"

Producing a lit pipe out of the air, Roger explained, "For many years now, all communication between us has been on the mental level." Pausing for effect, and to check that his companion had not fallen asleep, he explained, "On that level most of the personality and idiosyncratic traits we use in our daily dealings with each other was strained out or showed up only in our interpretations of pictures or images. Now I suppose we will have to get used to each other's little eccentricities."

Screwing his face muscles into something that resembled an aged pumpkin left out in the sun until it had fossilized, the thin man retorted, "*I* personally do not have any traits, strange ways, or eccentric things.... although I don't know about the rest of you!"

Holding back his reply, Roger folded his arms (or as close as he could get his arms to span across his vast chest and stomachs), pursed his lips, and sniffed the air before announcing, "Here comes Frank."

All at once another chair appeared. It hesitated a moment, and then disappeared again. Glancing at where it had been, Arnold said, "Frank!"

Roger nodded, enjoying his pipe too much to say more.

Suddenly, where the chair had materialized and disappeared, stood a tall, slim wizard with jet-black hair, moustache, beard, and eyebrows (all recently brushed). Roger nodded at Frank as another chair appeared to the left of Arnold. Who, although he was still holding his pumpkin face in as many wrinkles as possible, was able to watch as the chair settled itself on the ground with a small squeak. This chair was positively austere compared to the other two; it was made from dark wood and had no arms at all, only a long, straight, plain back with long legs and a much-used straw seat with nothing else. Frank looked at Francis's chair and moved his shoulders around as if they were new or did not fit very well. He slowly spelled back his own chair, feeling annoyed that Francis had spoilt his grand entrance.

Frank then walked over to his chair and sat on it as the air changed, indicating that magic was in use. An exceedingly tall and thin image slowly appeared out of nothing to become wizard Francis, the tallest, thinnest (and skeletal even comes to mind), of them all. He blinked, then sat on the edge of his seat and sniffed the air, glancing at his colleague before asking him, "Why is your face all screwed up, Arnold?"

Relaxing the muscles of his face, the small wizard confessed, "I was showing my disdain to Roger, and forgot to put it back. I was the first here, though."

Scratching his ear, Francis mumbled that Arnold always was the first, then asked, "Do we know how many have been found?"

Sitting forward, Arnold (the first) explained excitedly, "Amazingly, they have found one each! I didn't think they would do that well."

Francis, thinking of his beloved books, just smiled.

Frank looked around then asked "How many?"

"One each," Roger told him through a cloud of dark blue smoke.

Frank rubbed his nose thinking that if eight wizards had each brought back a pseudo apprentice then things would definitely be changing, "I have been wondering," he wondered aloud, "how many of them will really be worthy of teaching? Let alone how many of them will want to stay with us to learn? That is the real question."

Not asking what the unreal question would have been, while still happily puffing away on his pipe, Roger replied, "The more there are, the more chance there is that some of them will decide to stay."

Narrowing his dark eyebrows, Frank replied, "I doubt it! I really do! For you know that youngsters nowadays have no get up and go, and neither do they have any grit."

"Perhaps their get up and go has got up and gone, and

all of the grit has been eaten by the birds?" Roger observed and asked at the same time, using his pipe to point at the air in front of him.

Arnold ignored Roger and told Frank, "You always look on the dark side, Frank... shut up will you?... or I'll give you my face."

"Anything but that! Please forgive me, old face-giver," Frank said, snorting and shaking his head. Seeing that his sarcasm had gone unnoticed, Frank folded his arms and shook his head so much that the hat that sat on top of his head wobbled.

Francis snapped his fingers, making a loud, dry, earthy sound that got the attention of his fellow wizards. "Are you three going to be like this for all the time we will be talking?" he asked them.

Arnold sat straighter in his seat, waving his arms around as if he were conducting an orchestra, and spluttered a reply, "Like what? I am the first... and since you two have been here I have had nothing but insults and complaints, and... and where is Jack?"

"Complaints you say? You are the one who started it with your `I'm the first,'" Frank replied, allowing a small smile to cover his lips.

Roger replied that Jack was asleep as usual, then wobbling forward, he blew a lungful of smoke down at Arnold who pretended to cough. Then he really did cough going red and blue into the bargain, making Roger feel stupid for what he had done.

Frank waved his hands and then he disappeared, leaving his words to follow him as best they could, but taking his chair with him. "Call me when they arrive, will you...."

Francis blinked, then said that he had to write something down or he would forget it. He then asked that when they were calling Frank, could they please do the same for him kind of thing, as it really was terribly important that he was there to witness the first apprentice to arrive so that he could write it all down in his history book.

They nodded at him, then Francis and his chair disappeared, leaving just the two old friends quarrelling happily together.

Ten minutes later, Roger and Arnold were still happily arguing about which one of them was going to inform Frank and Francis, when they became aware that the first of the wizards would soon be arriving with one of the people that they hoped would end up an apprentice.

Roger sent a mental message to Frank and Francis. Frank appeared immediately, without his chair this time as he thought that he would look more powerful standing rather than sitting, and so had decided to leave it behind.

Then Francis's chair appeared and a second later so did Francis, who floated above it for a moment frowning until slowly he and his chair became one. Francis was looking at Frank who was carrying in his right hand a tall, carved staff. It was long and thin and quite dark, and shone in the afternoon sunshine, especially the small stone that was set at the top.

There is a saying amongst wizards that they grow to resemble their staffs rather than the staffs growing to resemble the wizards who carry them. This could be true based on the staffs that were on show: Roger's staff was short, blunt, and very, very wide; while Arnold owned a staff that was thin and twisted, and its surface was very rough to the touch. Francis's staff had two distinct bends in it and its carvings stood out proudly. He had not brought it today but was now wondering if he should go and get it as the others had all brought theirs. These staffs were the most personal and powerful thing a wizard owned, and anyone with any sense of self-preservation would not dare touch a wizard's staff even if they could, which would be most unlikely.

Many were the tales of some drunken fellow who, on staggering home late one night after visiting an inn, came upon a staff and on taking it in his hand was taken to another place and when he was brought back he had white hair and his family had all died, for he had been gone for so long.[9]

When a wizard died, he was supposed to choose who was to become the new owner of his staff (often one of his apprentices). If this did not happen, then the staff would choose a new owner itself, if it had enough stored spells and energy in it. If there was no one available or if it did not like its old wizard's choice (and seeing as its previous owner was dead and had no say in the matter of who was going to carry it all over the place) it would choose a new owner to accompany it for the next hundred years or so. As many wizards forgot to name a successor (as they did not have an apprentice) and as even the wizard's staffs could sometimes not find new owners, there soon became a build-up of un-

---

[9] This is a variation on the "getting old, getting drunk, and forgetting" story that many an old, drunk man quotes when he knows he is in the wrong, even though, as yet, there have never ever been any two wives who have believed the stories. In spite of this, most of the men still will come to believe them, especially when they have drunk a lot. The moral? Do not read footnotes - or at least do not expect them to explain everything or to always be interesting.

owned staffs and people who could hold them. These surplus staffs were kept far underground and under many spells to keep them under guard and to stop them going out looking for new owners (or worse still, to find their last ones). These mystical rods of magic and wood exchanged knowledge, gossiped, and waited staffly for something to happen and overall seemed quite happy.

Frank adjusted his tall, newly dusted hat, and said the obvious, "So, all the higher council is here except for Jack, Colin, and Douglas." A voice that had no body told them, "No... just Douglas and Jack are missing."

Then Colin's small, bent body appeared, with his stick-thin neck that always seemed too thin to support his large round head that bobbed up and down in greeting. He was smiling as he looked around, his dark, observant eyes and his dirty brown beard, moustache and hair all arranged themselves into the shape they usually took. He looked around and said, "Oops... no chair... silly me! Correction time is here." Then he flicked his fingers and his small, green leather-backed, dark wood-framed chair arrived, which he duly sat on.

Arnold asked him how he was - he asked only so that he could impress his fellow wizards with his manners and not from any desire to know the answer.

Colin got up from his seat and stood in front of Arnold saying, "One is not really sure quite how to answer that question. For a start, I have to ask... is it a real question that is related to a query where the answer is wanted, or is it just a way to acknowledge that the receiver is still alive? If you are asking how I am then I will need several points of reference before I could even start to formulate an answer.

Then I would need..."

He was stopped in mid-sentence by Roger who told him to leave some space for the rest of them, and then added that Arnold was just being polite.

Colin swallowed loudly and moved back to his seat, looking and feeling very meek. Francis crossed one of his long legs over the other and frowned, as he mentally struggled to find the sentence he would use to start his latest history book.

Frank spelled a seat for himself, then changed his mind and changed the seat into a stool, changed his mind again and spelled it into something he saw as more befitting: a long, slim, sparsely decorated, dark veneered, high backed and shiny chair. He pondered on how he would like to be seen by the others. Finally, he crossed his arms, containing his staff within their protection, and then asked, "Who will be the first?"

Arnold turned in his chair and explained that he had been the first as usual.

Frank said that he knew Arnold had been the first to arrive out of them for this meeting, but what he had meant was who was to be the first wizard to come back with a candidate?

Roger fluffed out his beard and settling one of his best scowls on his face, told them that the first of the wizards who had been searching had nearly arrived.

Then there was a shushing noise as the oldest wizard left in the known land appeared. This man was very small and at one time had even more wrinkles than Arnold, but as he kept on getting older they smoothed out, leaving him looking more over-ironed rather than wrinkled. His seat was a couch, complete with cushions and quilts and the odd sweet, cigarette packet, book, pen and many other odd objects concealed within its folds. Jack made Arnold look as young as a mere hundred (which he nearly was, come to think of it). The owner of this settee was the oldest and most knowledgeable of all the wizards, and he still had a few stubborn strands of white hair sticking up out of his mushroom-coloured pate. His beard was patchy and thin and a faded white grey in colour. His staff was unseen by anyone for years and Jack often joined it for long periods of time.

Peering at his colleagues, he attempted to wave his arm in greeting but gave it up as too much work, instead he gave them another smile to share between them, and went back to sleep.

Douglas (the only glasses-wearing and beardless wizard) appeared, and blinked a few times in greeting. Then he remembered that they were all supposed to talk to each other again and decided against the effort it would take. Instead, he nodded again, adjusted his thick-framed glasses, and looked in front of him.

Arnold pushed his eyebrows towards the heavens for a better view, reminded himself that at least he had been the first, and then reminded himself that they had all agreed to speak. He thought about telling them that he was still the first, but instead he just stared at the space in front of him where he was sure that the first returnee would return. He blinked a few times, shrugged his thin shoulders, then smiled until he was ready.

Roger rolled back in his chair and stared at the nothing in front of him, until he too was ready.

Frank finger combed his beard and prepared his face in that of a formal greeting, so that he too was now ready.

Colin walked around in a circle, shrugged, smiled, sat back down on his seat, and looked around expectantly and excitedly as he became ready.

Francis wrote in his head (to be transferred later to his beloved history book): "The high council assembled in readiness for the first person for fifty-eight years to arrive in Pearland to address the higher council as an applicant to become an apprentice."

# Chapter Eleven: The Arrivals

The first of the things they were all ready for came slowly into substance. It was Marcus, accompanying the tallest human the council had ever seen in their entire existence. This person was almost as thin as Francis but was much taller. He had lank brown hair that fell across his wide forehead and managed to do a good job of covering his two wide ears, which stuck out on either side of his round head.

From a distance, Tom looked like a half-sucked lollipop. He also looked like he was frozen in mid-sentence - which he was - for his mouth was open and his arms were hanging far out and away from his body. The small wizard at his side looked even smaller than normal in comparison to the long-boned young man to those of the council who were still awake and able to watch their arrival.

Marcus left the figure standing stock still and walked over to where his friends sat. Arnold was saying, "So, you are the first back. Well done, Marcus... I was the first here you know... Now, who have you brought for us to consider?"

Studying the ground at his feet, Marcus replied in a voice even quieter than usual. "This is a farmer's boy named Tom Daunt. He talks non stop, which is how I ended up with him for I couldn't tell him to go away or get away from him - for he wouldn't stop talking - so I brought him back. Sorry."

Roger made tutting sounds and pulled his mouth down;

Frank scratched his neck and smiled; Douglas formed a joke in his head and was just about to send an image of them changing Tom into a small animal, then he remembered the talking policy. He thought of trying to explain his thoughts and motivations in language alone, sighed at the effort, and so said nothing. Colin frowned, wondering if the boy's parents had both been tall or if the tallness had only come from one side of his ancestry. Then he wondered if the gene for tallness came about from some deficiency or some form of overabundance. Then he started to wonder if it was the same gene as the one that caused a lack of growth, then…. Francis tapped his lips in contemplation with his index finger while frowning; Jack snored softly at his side.

Even with all of these actions there was still a lot of room left for Arnold to say, "Well done, Marcus! A farmer's son - and one so tall and thin! He could learn to be an imposing figure, given the right incentive."

Marcus gave him a smile that told him how thankful he was for the comforting words but the end of the smile added that it knew Marcus had not done a very good job.

Roger told them that the boy probably had no idea what he really wanted, and that was why he talked so much.

Frank got to his feet, still holding his staff, and walked over to Tom. When he was standing in front of him he asked Marcus to release him.

Apologising, Marcus moved his hands and muttered the release spell.

Immediately Tom said, "So a-then the brown one a-saw the black one and... and…" (Marcus sighed in relief at the silence.) A few seconds later Tom said, "...Well how about that? Here I is - well, I mean... there I was - and now I am not a-there but a-here instead. Now if that a-don't beat a-square eggs! Hello, me a-name is Tom, and I am a-pleased to meet ya all." He moved up to Frank who was the nearest and still talking took his hand, squeezed it, and moved it vigorously up and down.

Then he turned to the other wizards and told them, "I am a-pleased to meet you all. Well, I a-have already a-met one of you! I am and a-was a mighty pleased to meet you then and still am now. So where be I - I'm a-wondering? It looks as if you a-folks don't get a-much rain in these parts. Soil looks dry; there are a few a-trees and bushes so there is water a-down there someplace - an all we have to do is to a-get it to come up to us or to a-get the roots a-down to it. The driest farm I ever a seen was that of the Yolkelsons, way up on the a-north ridge. Their dirt was the worse I a-come upon and in a-summer it was as dry as a fly, so what they a-did was to bring up water from a lake nearby. They did this for the first a-season or two then the ground a-sort of got the idea and a-started to keep more of the a-rain, a fine thing to a-see, yes indeed! I wonder if we could…."

Frank had been trying unsuccessfully to get a word in edgeways and, on losing the little patience he had, finally snapped his fingers, leaving Tom standing with his mouth open and his arms in mid-flight, almost the exact same position that he had been in when he had first arrived.

Frank shook his head in disgust as he walked back to the other wizards, wiping his hand on his robe. The rest of the wizards sat or (in Marcus's, Colin's, and Douglas's case) stood waiting.

Marcus apologised again saying that he knew he was not very good at that sort of thing and Arnold said that he was glad he did not have to train that tall boy. "I did not know he was Welsh?" Then, when no one reacted to his attempt at humour, Arnold went on to say, "Be fair Roger - he didn't really pick him as such. As I understand it he just couldn't get rid of him and anyway he may be all right with the right training - if he wants to - and... Marcus did his best and...."

He was saved from trying to find anything else positive to say by the appearance of a blonde haired and yellow bearded wizard. He had with him a small girl with multi-coloured hair who was dressed all in black, purple, and yellow. She somehow was able to clash most magnificently with herself.

Frank gasped, Arnold sighed, Colin tilted his head to one side, Francis wondered how he would describe her hair in his book, Douglas frowned, and Jack snored, leaving Roger to say, "Wilfred, so who have you got for us?"

Wilfred turned to the girl and said to her, "Not blank eyes, but with contact the faded who could slip you info on the cosmos if you are connected and direction focused." (They are all-seeing and have the power to help you learn how to become a wizard if you are committed and stay focused).

She looked the wizards up and down then asked, "Key fella - are you fitted? cos they come into my viewer as age dumped escapees." (I hear what you say. Is this a joke or are you for real? They look to me like ancient thrown away escapees.).

Nodding seriously, Wilfred replied, "Am I a triple sayer? No, this is cream on top and no guff levelled." (Am I a liar? No this is the best place to learn, they are the most powerful wizards, and I am not joking).

Frank snapped his fingers again to freeze her before she could reply. Douglas hid his smile, as Frank demanded of Wilfred, "What in the hall of blue blazes kind of language was that?"

Wilfred gave a simpering smile as he explained in his normal voice, "I believe they call it kid-speak, it does have a certain flow and charm of its own. Although I will grant you that it does also grate at first but after a short while, especially after you have understood some of its little ways, it does the job of communicating in a distinct and unique way. It definitely does have an interesting way of getting to the point especially when the..." He stopped as Arnold squashed his features into one of his faces, showing to the world at large that he was deep in thought.

Roger asked Wilfred, "I really hope you do not expect *us* to learn this speak kid?" Frank tutted in a superior way then glanced at each of his colleagues as he was waiting for his obvious observation to become clear to them. Colin played with a tassel on the cushion of his chair; Francis mentally tried to write down the unusual description of the young girl while Jack snored peacefully. Douglas adjusted his thick, black-framed glasses while Roger scratched at his left ear.

Arnold un-squashed his face and started to speak but Roger cut him short, much to Arnold's annoyance, "So, we have one boy who does not stop talking or care to listen, and one girl who speaks a language that is neither one thing nor the other. Quite a pair really, all things considered."

Douglas spoke for the first time, feeling that he had no other choice. "Maybe she can learn ta speak oor language?" he suggested delicately, pushing his glasses higher up the bridge of his nose. Everyone ignored him, except Jack, who snored a little louder in agreement. Wilfred shrugged his shoulders, saying that she was definitely the best in the whole school. Douglas nodded, just being glad that he had not had to go out there to look for any apprentices. Frank raised his eyebrows, looking like a chicken that wanted its neck chopped, but he was ignored again as Roger said that it must have been quite a school.

Wilfred replied that it mostly took students whose parents could afford to pay. Roger nodded as he said that would explain everything.

Frank said as loudly as he could, while still keeping his decorum[10], "I can't wait for the next wizard to appear – who knows? He might have somebody with him who talks our language, listens perhaps, and maybe could even be asked to stop talking if the need ever arose? Not that there isn't anything else wrong."

Douglas smiled to himself as he watched Frank twitch even more, making Douglas think that he was even worse now that he used words than when he used wizard telepathy. Francis moved his lips as he mentally wrote down the scene in front of him. Colin coughed to cover his laughter as Roger took a lungful of air then slowly released it as the next wizard came into view.

The large, solid shape of Bill appeared before them. He had a blonde girl with him dressed in a shapeless costume with faded numbers on it that did nothing to hide most of her muscles. She looked around her and her jaw fell open; then, on seeing the old men, she tensed her muscles and pasted a fierce and defiant look on her pretty face. Frank felt

---

[10] I do not know where he kept it, on his person I suppose.

glad that he was so far away from her. He folded his arms, setting his thin lips even thinner and twitched like a twitch machine on overtime to cover up his true feelings. He acted like a bird watcher who has seen a rare bird and just as it lands, someone walks in front of his vision to scare it away.

Arnold leant forward for a better look and grinned evilly, Roger pursed his lips in preparation of making an observation or two but all he did was stare. Colin covered his mouth and went even redder with the effort of holding back his laughter. Jack snored on; Marcus smiled at Bill and then looked at the striking form of the young woman (well, she would strike anyone if she found the need to, believe me) and moved behind Roger. Francis gave Bill a small wave of recognition as he indicated with his head the static figure of Tom and the hair-girl (as he thought of her) who stood just behind them. Bill glanced at them as Jack made a slurping sound in his sleep - that could mean anything or nothing, but probably meant both. Douglas put his hand to his chin to help keep his jaw closed but failed to keep two words from escaping, "Och dear!"

The girl looked at the strange old men then back at the two statue figures to her right. She shifted her weight to her right foot in case she needed the purchase to suddenly move very quickly away from them.

"May I introduce you to the council of wizards?" Bill said to her. "These learned gentlemen could teach you some of the things you may wish to acquire in the way of knowledge, so that you will never be at anyone's mercy again."

She stayed where she was as Bill pointed to each of his learned fellow wizards saying, "This chap is Arnold, the round one next to him is Roger. Frank is the one with the hat; the tall one is Francis, he is even tall when he is sitting down but I see that the blonde youth is even taller than he is, makes me wonder - and that? That small one hiding behind Roger is Marcus; Douglas is the one with the glasses; the small dark one is Colin; the blonde one is Wilfred and the one asleep is Jack. They are in fact my friends, the wizards."

She pivoted on the balls of her feet until she was facing him directly, then she asked in a voice full of disbelief, "You are all wizards? I thought you were just stories, or at least that you were all long dead."

Bill nodded at her statement, examining it on both sides, then on the inside and finally at both ends. When he had finished he nodded, ready to explain, "We do not need to deal with people very often as we spend our time studying the ancient art of magic. Which suits us, and it makes our lives easier if those few who we do meet think we are not wizards, because then they leave us alone - and that."

Frank snapped his fingers and her reply was lost as she joined Tom and the kid-speaker in frozen action. Bill stood facing his companions, giving Frank a look that said he should have been the one to still her - and that. Then he moved across the short distance to join them.

# Chapter Twelve: Mixed Wizards

As Bill came to stand next to Roger, Frank stood up and tried to look important. In fact, he just looked like a Frank who had become a bit stiffer than usual; he also looked as if he was on stage and had forgotten his opening words. He moved in front of the wizards, with his back to the frozen guests, where they could all see him.

Once he was sure he had their undivided attention he asked, "Does not something strike you learned gentlemen - my brother wizards - something about two of these wondrous people who have been brought here to learn our ways?" He paused just long enough to see if anyone had any idea what he was indicating - and on seeing that they had none he smiled happily and nodded before saying, "Is there not something about two of these three that you are considering making into WIZARDS?"

Frank said the word WIZARD in capital letters, hoping this would give them a clue as to his meaning but again he was happily disappointed. Looking at the blank faces that stared at him from their various positions, he saw that they did not have a clue about what was so obvious to him. Having this information and with as much fuss and histrionics as he could muster and acting as hammy as a herd of fat old porkers, he stroked his jet-black beard as he explained, "Those proverbial apprentices that you went so far to find," he twirled and pointed at the two females.

"These wonderful young people who could be the answer to the complicated problem of finding a reason to continue our life's work, and to hand down our combined knowledge to on a plate." He took another lungful of air then continued, "These people who are going to make our lives worthwhile. Who are to be the vessels of our combined knowledge, the answer to all of our problems, and the next founder generation of wizardry, in this fair land of ours, these people!" He studied his audience as he finally got to the point.

"Now, can you not see a small problem? Is there not something that you should notice about them?" Frank turned back to face them and leant backwards as he swung his arms as far from his sides as possible as he told them, "These wonderful young intelligent vessels of people who are..." He glanced at the assembled wizards who sat and waited for they had nothing better to do at the time. Then changing his mind in mid-flight he told them, "The first thing I noticed about TWO of the much sought after applicants..." he underlined the number two by sticking two fingers up in front of his face. "Not one... but two... notice, TWO of the three new empty knowledge seekers are..." He paused for as long as he could, judging it just long enough for them not to fall asleep or to go on without him, until finally he finished "…FEMALE! I will say it once again…Female! WE are WIZARDS and we are all MALE... get it? Wizards are MALE, wizards have always been male, always, since the dawn of time. And there is a rule that says wizards are male, men not women, boys not girls - and not women or female in anyway at all. Those two are FEMALE... AND FEMALES DO NOT BECOME WIZARDS!"

He stuck his head back, folded his arms across his chest, and waited for the applause, or at least their grovelling acceptance at the obvious point they had missed so completely.

Instead of applause or even congratulations, the wizards sat or stood scratching their beards or other areas of themselves and avoiding each other's eyes until finally Roger summed up their thoughts and feelings, "So... that is that then, I suppose."

Arnold looked at Frank's superior sneer and added, "Well, what I want to know is - what reasons are there that wizards are always men?"

Frank opened his eyes in surprise as some of the other wizards started to nod in agreement.

Hiding his smile, Arnold said, "I don't know any reasons why girls cannot become wizards. Do you? I wonder if it is just some stupid rule or other, or something that started long ago when the women had better things to do at the time, so it just became habit to only take men."

Frank opened his eyes to their fullest then walked to where the three figures remained like statues and used them to demonstrate his points. "It has nothing to do with rules but much more to do with something (or some things) that cannot be changed," he explained. "...In spite of your desperate needs," he added, as sarcastically as he was able. He reached up and tapped Tom on the forehead as he continued, "This is a male. Note the energy field, it goes around him, there are areas where it gathers and areas where energy is stored. This is in fact a sealed unit of energy, and once the energy or rituals and knowledge are inside of an energy field it stays there. A sealed unit, a male sealed unit, a male that should go on to become a man... a man like what we all are... men! Male units are not open in any real way for the energy to escape or for the energy that surrounds it to contaminate it. It is closed... locked... and not open in any way."

He moved a few steps to where the other two applicants stood equally frozen before saying, "Now we come to these two." He waved his hand in front of the two females but as far away from their bodies as he could while still indicating them. He was being careful not to get too close for fear of contamination, as he explained, "Again, study their energy fields and what do we notice?" Frank allowed the briefest of smiles to lie on his lips as he drew in as much air as his ancient lungs would allow, then screamed, "We notice that their energy field is not completely contained! It is in actual fact an OPEN energy field. For anatomical reasons they have a... a... connection with the other energies that flow around them. It has an outlet. This is not a sealed unit, and so any spells and knowledge would flow out of it and not be contained in any way at all!"

He stepped away from the females and closer to his audience telling them, "That, gentleman, is why they are used in other forms of knowledge and magic; knowledge that needs, or at least incorporates, the energy flow of the local area. These are females such as the wiccans, wise women, herb givers, and of course witches... that sort of thing. They are females and I would even go as far as to say that they are ideally suited for the kind of positions that use open energy around them as they move around. MEN on the other hand are ideally suited for contained energy field magic. They have the ability to store energy! That is why 'male men' are magicians and WIZARDS! Do I make myself clear, gentlemen?"

A long, sad silence lasted and Frank listened to it with his eyes closed and a triumphant smile widening with every moment.

Roger finally broke it saying, "Thank you, Frank." Then after a while added, "So... that is that then." He said this gruffly, while staring at the two girls and feeling glad that it was not he who would have to return them to their environments.

"Technically speaking, both sexes are different but both benefit equally well from their differences," said Francis.

Arnold frowned, deep in thought, then in a determined voice said, "That does not seem very fair to me. I mean, to dismiss them just like that, for they do have exceptional spirits and their energy is fine, is there no way we could teach them something?"

Wilfred held up his hand, stopping the conversation, a most unusual thing for him to do. Then, standing up to his full height and nearly coming up to Frank's chest, he began, "It didn't occur to me at the time that mine was a girl. What was obvious to me was that not only did she have the right spirit and attitude to become a wizard, but also that she has more need than anyone I have ever met. I have thought about what you said, Frank, but I have to agree with Arnold. There must be some way we can help her to use our kind of energy and magic. I feel I owe it to... to... whatever her name is, to at least try to keep my promise of putting her forward for candidacy."

Bill slapped him on the back, causing a cloud of dust to float angrily around and forcing Wilfred to take two involuntary steps forward to avoid falling onto his face. Bill said, "I agree! The girl I brought back came from the slave pens and has been a slave for over a year. A year! Can you imagine what that must have been like for her - and that?"

Arnold tried to speak but failed, as he was able to imagine one small part of what it must have been like for her and immediately felt guilty at his first response to her. Roger started a sentence but thought better of it. Francis searched his memory for female wizards in all of the wizarding records he had ever read and failed to find any. Jack grinned in his sleep. Douglas thought about energy fields in animals and then mammals and finally insects. Arnold tried not to think about the slave girl and all that she had endured in her short life in an attempt to stop the tears from pouring from his eyes and, when this failed, he did a quick-change spell, then felt marginally better. Colin thought of all the female magic users he had known and then wondered if their spirit connection was just to the mind or to the body as well. Wilfred closed his eyes until he felt better; Marcus shook his head in despair[11] and Frank shivered at the concept of female wizards - and females in general cluttering the place up - but he felt proud to have been the only one to see and point out the potential problem.

In a clear voice, Bill told them, "I didn't notice that she was female. Well, I noticed - but I didn't see it as a problem, which was stupid of me. I chose her as she not only had the best reason and energy, but because she had the best spirit and intelligence of anyone else in the entire area. I want to do whatever I can to help her and unless the council forbids

---

[11] He did not actually go there but sort of brought despair to him.

it then I will do everything that I can for her, in any way that I can - and that."

Jack opened his eyes, which had the same effect as Frank clapping his hands, or Arnold shouting, or Roger rolling out of his chair, or Colin doing a handstand or Douglas growing a beard and getting rid of his glasses. All wizard eyes settled on Jack, who was the oldest, the most knowledgeable, and the most influential of them all (when he was awake that is). He moved in his chair, and, with a voice that was as thin and high as a breeze, said, "If there is one thing we have learnt in our many years of study, it is that nothing is static." He took a few deep breaths before he could say, "For life to continue it must be able to change; for all life is in constant flux or it will start to die, isn't that right, Francis?"

Francis nodded his head, frowned and pursed his lips as Jack again filled his ancient lungs with more fresh air, then continued, "All of the many other groups and civilizations that have tried to keep their blood and customs pure (as they perceived it) have failed, and most of them have died out. They failed because without change and growth there is only decay. Why are there so few of us wizards left in the land? A perfect example, I think."

Francis coughed loudly, then as they all stared at him he got to his feet, telling them, "You are definitely right, Jack. We tried, as many people have done in the past, to concentrate on the areas we thought were the most productive and on the things that we liked the best. We each chose the part of wizardry that we liked the most, and now we have become a dying breed." He looked around as he said, "I know of no female wizards in any of my books - but that does not mean there has never been one - or that there can never be any. Let us do what we can for those who want to follow our path, male or female, for I believe that we must be open to change or face the consequences, as Jack has so eloquently pointed out." He stopped and felt weak after talking so loud and with such conviction. He sat back down, hoping that no one would ask him anything for a long while.

Studying him as if from a new angle, the other wizards (except for Frank) told him that they were all in agreement with his observations - not as passionately as he was, but then he did read a lot.

Frank scratched his left ear, glanced at the two young people who were at the heart of the conversation, and finally said, "All right then... if you think you can go against nature and hundreds of years of history, who am I to try and stop you? I wish you all of the luck in the land. It could be a worthy task now that I come to think of it... yes, let us try! It is the least and the most we can do and if it will mean the end of us all then who am I to complain or stand in your way?"

Arnold tried to construct a sentence about how Frank was the exact opposite of someone who keeps optimistic even under extreme conditions, but he failed... so he kept quiet.

The council spent the next few minutes congratulating each other on their decision, while ignoring Frank and his sarcasm, until the next wizard appeared, stopping all conversation as their curiosity overcame them. They smiled as the air thickened, indicating the approach of another wizard; they each wondered who it would be, whom they would have with them and whether they would be male or female.

Soon they saw Reginald and heard a small youth who looked as though he had been fed to a couple of toothless dragons who had eventually spat him out after gumming him for a few days. He was saying, "Oh great one, I am not worthy. I will dedicate my life to seeing thine temple is kept clean and that the worshippers…." The owner of the voice stopped in mid speech (quite an achievement for him) at the sight of the frozen figures and lack of mountain. Blinking, he shook his head, glanced around, saw the group of old bearded men and promptly turned around, throwing himself face down onto the hard ground in front of them.

Reginald sighed, then bent to pick him up as he tried to explain where he was, "Dear boy there... er... really is no need for you to... um... do that. You will hurt yourself. This is... um... where we live. If you... er..., really wish to stay we will find somewhere for you to... um... stay also. These good souls are... er... my friends, and they are not gods or spirits but... um... just plain old everyday wizards."

The boy wriggled out of Reginald's hands, flopped to his knees again and began to explain that he was not worthy, but Reginald spelled him still. Then, making a chair from some of the loose energy that the boy had expended, Reginald sat down heavily on it as he explained that the boy had taken his way of talking from storybooks and that it had become a bit of a habit with him. He then told them how the youth had climbed a mountain to seek knowledge from the mountain god.

Frank nodded as he said, "Now, this one sounds like just the stuff we need... a real chip off the old block. But I do not like to be called a plain everyday wizard, though."

Arnold suddenly made a strange noise. Everyone who

was capable, everyone that is except for Jack who did not need to, turned to look at him and stared. It took them a while to turn the sound into something that they recognized - he was laughing! Finally, he gained enough control to explain the reason for his sudden unusual mirth, "Sorry, chaps, it was the mental image of Frank climbing a mountain that filled me with humour, can you imagine it?"

All eyes that were capable of moving, including the right one of Jack's, focused on the lank, skinny form of Frank. All of them started to smile and a few chuckled as Arnold wheezed happily while even Jack snorted a laugh or two.

Frank said in his own defence, "When I said that he was a chip off the old block, I didn't mean that I had climbed mountains - only that he was a seeker as we were... er... are."

Jack furrowed his brow to aid his memory and opened his left eye to give his right one a rest as he recalled, "When you arrived, Frank, it was with old Marcia. I remember now! You thought that once you learnt how to use magic you could control all the women you blamed for all your past mistakes."

Frank moved closer to the prone figure, waving his hands as his eyes got larger and larger and his face redder as he said, "We do not need to go into that now, Jack. I was young and naive: this boy still seems the best by far to me – that's the point I was trying to make."

It was the first time most of them had seen Frank any colour except his normal olive colouring. His red face shone hotly as he pretended nothing was happening.

Jack said, just loud enough for Arnold (who was next to him) to hear, "I remember how you were when you arrived - young Arnold as well... you had few a strange ideas of your own, I seem to remember."

Bill came to Arnold's rescue, mainly because he was frightening himself with what Jack might say about him next, saying, "From what little I can tell from these chosen ones..." he indicated the frozen figures, "...Frank could be right, if only we can get him to be honest and talk a little more normally like us - and that."

They agreed and nodded as only wizards can nod. Their conversation was interrupted by the voice of Henry who even as he appeared was saying, "Damn! Now, who left those strays in my way, could have been a nasty accident," then as he became solid said, "Hi other wizards, miss me?"

The small dark wet boy, who stood at his side and held himself stiffly, studied the group of ancient magicians before him. He started to shiver, unsure if he was dreaming or if this was all real. Henry wiped his long beard with the back of his hand as he explained to the group, "Found this young guy at that monastery place. He was the only one who showed any real spirit and guts so I thought he should have a chance. Anyone for a coffee?"

Seeing the fear and confusion in the boy's energy field, and his wide-open eyes, Wilfred walked over and bent down so that his face was level with him. Then he explained to the child, "We are all wizards, and we want to know if you would like to be put forward to become one of our apprentices or not? It's really up to you, you know - but there is nothing to fear from us... there really is nothing to fear."

Swallowing dryly, the terrified boy replied, "Are you really wizards? Not monks in disguise?"

Over his many years, Wilfred had been thought of as

many things: small, cheap, Scandinavian, stupid, ignorant, intrusive, Swedish, pushy, German, American, kind, helpful, trustworthy and (on one occasion) an excellent student - but never a monk.

Frowning, he explained to the boy in as reassuring a voice as he could find, "I assure you that we have nothing to do with monks and never have as far as I know, their ways are not ours. We are wizards, we have beards - and look - that one over there even has a pointed hat." Wilfred pointed at Frank who stood to attention now that the spotlight was finally on him for the right reason.

Holding the boy's frightened eyes with his own kind ones, Wilfred smiled at him as he noticed that the boy was shivering and soaking wet. He sent a glance back over his shoulder at Henry, indicating that he should not have left him wet, but he was deep in conversation with Roger, so Wilfred spelled the boy dry before explaining that he was safe here with them for as long as he wanted to stay. "We will not hurt you or force you to do anything you do not want to do," he added. "Most of us will treat you as a person and no one will treat you any less than you deserve to be treated. How we do treat you will to some extent depend on how you behave towards us. Some of them may be impolite or gruff but then they treat everyone the same way, and so there you are. If you want to take up this position and the council accepts you, then you will have to do as they say, but then that is so that you can continue to live and learn amongst us. Now, are you tired or hungry, by the way?"

The small head went slowly up and down, so Wilfred led him near, but not too near, the other wizards; then he produced a wooden bench for them to sit on. Wilfred and the boy sat talking quietly, leaving Henry still discussing his find and sipping his coffee.

Frank grinned at the young boy who moved even closer to Wilfred and as far away from Frank's stare as it was possible to get without causing offence. Francis observed that Frank was happy again and had changed his mind about who the best candidate was now that this small dark boy had arrived.

Frank told his colleagues, "Two, two of them, that is more than I had hoped for. Good. I am now hopeful."

Out of earshot of the wizards, the boy mustered up the courage to ask Wilfred a question as the other wizards's attention turned to face the next two figures who were materializing in front of the row of still unmoving youths.

"It's Joe!" Arnold told them unnecessarily, as the comfortable well-worn form of Joe appeared, dwarfed by a girl with bright yellow hair who held her large hands to her face in defiance of the journey.

She was dressed in an unmarried farmer's going-out-with-little-hope-left clothes, a dress that went close to the ground without actually touching it while at the same time keeping as far away from her body as it could, thus keeping her true shape a secret while somehow still allowing maximum movement and protection. Over this, she wore a white garment with many flowers embroidered on it and a large pocket set at an angle over her stomach. On her feet were a pair of worn brown boots that would be too big even for Roger and in her hair was a lost comb.

Joe indicated her with a tilt of his head, saying, "How's this, any good? Anyway, I'm tired and fed up of looking so it will have to do." Then he walked over to the bench where

Wilfred and the boy sat talking softly and sat down heavily on the opposite end. The girl stroked her thick tresses down the side of her head as she looked around as coyly as possible under her present circumstance, first at the old men then slowly at the unmoving figures around her.

When she saw Tom, she gasped in surprise at a vision she had been dreaming of since she was only a few summers old. *Was this a dream*? she asked herself, then she pinched herself to check, but before she was able to receive the information of pain or no pain, Roger froze her in mid-pinch.

"Why did you do that?" asked Joe gruffly.

Roger explained, "I didn't want her to hurt herself and anyway I was getting fed up waiting for you to do it."

Looking around, Joe said, "Oh, sorry, I didn't notice that you had spelled them all still." He produced a cigarette from out of the air then puffed on it before saying, "I don't think much of this talking lark, do you? Whom are we waiting for anyway?"

Roger made a show of counting on his fingers as he replied. "Wilfred is talking to the one Henry brought from the monastery, Marcus is there, Bill and you are here and there is Reginald, that means we are just awaiting the arrival of Albert and Martin."

Arnold tutted at the explanation, secretly wishing he had said it first.

"Maybe they could not find anyone?" Roger suggested, still beaming at his latest success of beating his friend to the explanation.

"Trust you to look on the dark side," was the best that Arnold could do before Martin became solid enough to be able to smile at them.

He was holding the hand of a small round red-faced child who was little more than a baby and who had the reddest hair any of them had ever seen in their entire lives. Even in Jack's long life he had never encountered hair as red as this. It was the brightest of bright reds with no gold or yellow or ginger amongst it, as is usual in many people with red hair. This one was just red and very, very red at that.

Looking down at her, Martin smiled, then explained to the wizards, "I found this poor child in the city castle place. She is really quite nice; her name is, or was, Follia, it was written on the end of her bed." Giving the child's hand a gentle squeeze, he explained to her that he was going to put her to bed for a while so that he could talk to his fellow wizards. A bed appeared and she climbed up on it; then as he tucked her under the warm covers he produced a teddy bear that he put under her fat arm before spelling her to sleep.

"What were you thinking? That we have a nursery? Or perhaps that we should start one – just for your offering?" Frank asked Martin.

Martin explained that although she was young, she had a strong presence with an abundance of energy. This was one of the reasons the other children had bullied her, and her life would not have got any better - and so she needed and deserved a chance. Then, stopping any more questions by a wave of his hand he explained, "By the way, at the city castle I met a magician by the name of Algernon. He even has an apprentice, and was very helpful. He even gave me a meal then showed me where to look for an applicant."

Gasps and other such sounds of surprise came from all

the wizards at the news of a surviving magician. Arnold suggested that he would like to meet him; but Roger reminded him that they had something else to do first: sort out the apprentices from those who did not want, could not do, or were not good enough from the ones that they might be able to teach. Arnold thanked him (much to Roger's surprise), then asked him to remind him about visiting this Algernon sometime in the future. Jack peered from under his wrinkled brow remembering all the magicians he had known over his long life. Francis was so surprised at hearing that there were still magicians left alive that he could only nod as he mentally started a new chapter in his history book, and then wondered if it should be started with a footnote. Douglas wondered what all the fuss was about, as did Colin, who was watching the red-haired child as she sucked on the teddy bear's ear in her sleep. Frank thought of all the problems that the baby would give them and just smiled happily, crossing his arms and legs and gently nodding his head.

Martin told them that she had the best spirit he had seen in any of the residents of the castle city. Frank shook his head and looked up at the sky as Marcus hid behind Roger, leaving Francis to tell them about all the famous red-haired wizards there had ever been, making Martin grin and nod at him.

Then the air changed again, indicating that something was going to appear.

# Chapter Thirteen: Feast of Apprentices

The wizards turned to look at the space where they each knew someone was about to appear. Albert came into sight holding onto another small, frightened child. He looked around at the other children and pulled his mouth downwards, indicating that he was more impressed than he cared to admit at there being so many candidates. Then he looked at the wizards and smiled as he told them, "Hold on there... just telling him what he needs to know... then I will be with you." He nodded at the child as he tried to explain to him what had happened and that he was going to be presented as a candidate to become a wizard's apprentice.

Albert shook his head and tutted as he created an information spell that he sent towards the child. When he had finished he again nodded, and the boy eyes and mouth were as open as he could make them from shock, surprise, and hope - in that order. Albert nodded at him yet again then said very slowly, "You stay here with the others while I go and talk to my friends... okay?"

The boy understood some of the words by the shape of the old man's mouth, such as *you here* and *go,* but not the rest. He received more information from watching how the old man glanced at the other young people and then tilted his head at the other old men, which allowed him to work out that he was like the other young people, and that the wizard was going to talk with the other old men.

As Albert started to walk towards the wizards, Frank said in a loud, sneering voice, "Albert, have you not noticed that all of the others are spelled still? Why is not yours?"

"'Cos I did not know, is why... as you well know."

They glared at each other until Roger said, "Well, someone should still the poor boy."

Albert snapped his fingers and the youth became still.

"Welcome back, Albert. How ya doing?"

Albert looked at Wilfred and smiled, replying that he had covered a lot of ground, was feeling a bit tired, and thank you for asking.

With Frank standing with his arms folded, the rest of the wizards broke into small groups and started to chat happily until they heard, "I was the first - and now am going to be the first to ask if we are going to see them moving?" Arnold told them and asked at the same time (showing that he was not just the first but had talent as well).

The wizards looked at each other to see if any of them had any further reasons to keep the applicants frozen. Roger sent out some soothing and confidence spells to help them adjust to their new environment as the other wizards agreed that there was no reason to wait any longer and so used various spells to free their visitors.

Even as the stilling spells were still going away (for a well-deserved rest), Tom started talking. He looked around at the rest of the youths who seemed to have appeared from nowhere before saying, "...Make some form of pond or water holder and a-then you a...." He paused and grinned as he looked at each of them in turn saying, "Well a-looky here! Welcome there folks, Tom is ma name and I am a-farmer but if I will always a-be one I..."

As he was saying this Mountain Boy (as the wizards had named him) bowed, hiding his true feelings and facing the old men. "Thou are indeed the greatest and most wondrous creators of myth and fabled legend..."

The girl with the many colours in her hair stepped back saying, "Whoa my holder" (Stop my heart) "wobble maker rules" (Unsure of my situation) "want a thing totally without freedom from platform view" (I require something solid to hold on to so that I can take in the new situation). She looked at the other candidates, taking a deep breath as she studied them. Finally, shaking her head she looked across at the wizard who had brought her and told him, "You think I am going to gel with glogs like these?" (Do you think that I am going to work with deficient inferior low lives like these?) "...you must be a rice can." (Then you must be mistaken and more inferior in your thoughts and understanding than I thought you were). "Yet, the put in was a light and radiated the most." (Mind you, the way that you made them arrive out of nowhere was quite impressive).

Before Wilfred could respond, the tall figure of Tom moved past her and over to the mountain boy, asking, "I am a-wondering a-how we can get this a-here soil to take up more water... any ideas? I was a-wondering if you be a farmer as well but a-then I see that you are a-dressed for something else. Maybe it was a-party or maybe your folks always a-dress that way or maybe it was because you a-had a hog of a job and was a-saving your best or normal for... for..." He suddenly lost the power of speech as he caught sight of the tall girl with the yellow hair who stood watching him from the end of the line.

She had been studying him as though he was a new

species that she was interested in obtaining. To most people she looked like a tall, very solid, shy girl with long thick hair and a face to match, but to Tom she looked like every farm boy's dream (which in a way she was). She stood holding her hands in her lap[12] and moving her body in half circles without moving her feet. To Tom, she encompassed farm-ability, femininity and wife-ability - in that order - and he instantly fell head over heels in love with her.

Tara had spent the time while this was going on accepting her new reality. She looked around her, blinked a few times and then got angry. To her, Myrtle's swaying movements meant servitude so she stepped forward to stand in front of her trying to block her from Tom's view. She yelled up into the yellow-haired female's wide face. "You do not have to fawn to anyone anymore! We are free."

Compressing her lips, the tall blonde farmer put her hands on her hips, and looking down deep into Tara's eyes, whispering, "I saws him first, he's mine and I'll fights far him if I have ta."

Surprise made the ex-slave step back and she followed the girl's stare over to Tom who she was still watching from under her eyelashes.

Tara then understood that Myrtle simply wanted to be his friend, so shaking her head the ex-slave muttered something under her breath and stepped away. She then noticed a small child sitting up in the bed and doing her best not to cry. She went over to her and sat on edge of the bed asking if she needed anything.

The red-lidded eyes moved across Tara's face until they

---

[12] You had to be there really to see how she had a lap when she was standing up - it was strange - but then so was she to many people and they to her.

found her eyes, then in a small frail voice the child asked, "Wan man?" As she said this, she waved her arms out in front of her indicating that she wanted physical contact with someone.

Realising that she must mean someone she knew, Tara looked around reasoning that this child had arrived, as she had, with a wizard. She pointed to where all of them stood or sat.

A small red smile crawled across the fat face as she recognised Martin amongst the other strange men and she started to crawl along the bed towards him.

Tara waved her hand to catch Martin's eye and he came over to stand smiling down at the chubby red-haired child, and then bent over to pick her up in his arms although he quickly sat down on the bed before he dropped her. A combination of lack of exercise on his behalf and an abundance of size on hers prohibited him from holding her in a standing position longer than a few seconds. Therefore, Martin sat with her on the bed talking quietly to her as they both started the process of getting used to each other in preparation for their new future together.

While this was happening, a thatch of multi-coloured hair waved in the breeze as its owner stood looking at the dark-eyed boy who glared back at her in response. Her hand tightened on her satchel as she studied him for a moment; then, hoping that she may have found a real (in her terms) person to talk to, she asked him, "Previous personnel you?" (Do you have any information or ideas about the situation here?)

He frowned and stiffened as he held her gaze, asking, "What did you say?"

"Before background yours?" (Where did you come from?)

Still frowning, the boy looked at the girl, saying, "I am here because a wizard brought me. Is this a test?"

Grinning, Gloria replied that he was, "filled without a lid, before is rusted, and faded then. Come you where?" (You are open to influences without taking the responsibility of the knowledge learnt. It would seem to me that a lot of what I have learnt and known is not relevant or helpful to me in this situation. Where did you come from?)

Giving the strange looking girl a fearful look, he replied to the only part of the sentence that he had understood. "I come from a small village. Are you a wizard?"

Shaking her head and making her hair swirl, she explained, "Empty area me. I am here to swim in smoke maker and skull fill." (No, I am here to work with the wizard and learn everything that I can from him).

"I don't know what you are saying... why do you speak like that and do you have to?"

"Kid-speak are royalty words and are topper." (Kid-speak is the best and most prodigious way to speak.)

"Kid-speak? What is that?" he asked, wondering if she was making fun of him.

"Wind-blown and no corner strapped! Only way to keep the non-knowers from laying buckles or nails."

Frowning, Keryon thought about her words, then told her his interpretations of them. "Wind-blown must mean moving around... and buckles hold things in place... so you must mean free, right?"

"Cigar! Keep doogs and skulls away."

He wanted to say, "By using words most people don't

use you think that you are free to talk about them without them knowing what you are saying, right?" Instead, he said, "You are hiding like?"

"Crown-wearer is you." (A compliment saying that he had reached a high level of understanding.) She said this while moving her eyes quickly from side to side looking at the other candidates.

"Do you know who these other people are?" asked Keryon, hoping that he had passed the test.

"One packed me."

Sighing, he tried to untangle her words but failed. So he missed "Pack" = to put into something with other things, "me" = description added together should mean that they were all brought to this place.

She folded her arms and stood smiling at him until he suddenly had an inspirational thought, "You mean we are all here for the same reason - that the wizards brought us all here!"

"Winner you a ticket holder to the main event." (You have successfully understood and now are able to talk with me about them as I have given you permission.)

Again ignoring her words, he revealed, "Henry brought me here - and told me that he would put me before something to see if it would take me; and that other one was kind." He pointed to Wilfred, making her tell him that he was wrong tracking (making a mistake).

Keryon did not understand her words, only her annoyance, and so acted towards it. "That one brought me and that one made me dry."

Waving her multi-coloured mane of hair, the girl told him, "Smoke trainer glove me." (The wizard who found me is to be my teacher alone.)

"Why don't you speak normal?"

"Small hat squeak like rats," she replied (Head is beginning to hurt, won't you talk normal?).

Thc boy shrugged his skinny shoulders as she asked him, "Kid-speak filled you?"

He shook his head, telling her that he was tired and hungry and couldn't be bothered to work so hard and if she couldn't be bothered to talk normally then he wouldn't be bothered to talk to her at all.

"Soft filling you and crammed tight." (You are filled with your own ways only) she told him, grinning happily.

"Shut up and leave me alone!" He snapped at her, stepping away.

"Sour pit with bugs and worms no sticky." (You are in a very bad state of being and see if I care anyway).

They moved apart, scowling at each other, wondering what would happen next. Not far from them, the ragged form of the boy who had climbed the mountain still knelt and prayed silently to the strange gods who held his fate in their wrinkled hands.

Bill smiled over at the female he had rescued from slavery. She made a move towards him, but he indicated that she should wait for a while if she would be so kind. She stopped - but only because she wanted to (her look told him and anyone else who was watching) and not because he had asked her.

Then Tara noticed a small, thin boy dressed in a green and brown garment who was staring around him with large frightened eyes. She moved over to him, then asked his name.

The terrified boy stared at her in silence as she repeated the question. This time the boy said in a throaty voice, "Mocker name me."

"Unusual name that," she told him with a frown. "Where have you come from?"

Again, the boy stared at her face and she saw the fear and confusion fill his eyes, making her determined to do whatever she could to remove it. "Don't be scared," she told him, "I won't let anyone hurt you."

He nodded, but she didn't think that he believed her or that he could understand her. "Is there anything I can do to help?" Tara asked him.

Frowning, the boy tried to make her lip movements into words he could understand.

Tara was starting to wonder if he was all there when she suddenly slapped the palm of her hand on her forehead, frightening the boy and making him jump involuntarily. Then he stared at her as she tapped her ear with two fingers. In response to her question he smiled and shrugged then he put his head on one side.

"Are you deaf?" she asked him slowly but without exaggerating her lip movements.

His smile broadened and he nodded his head so hard he nearly shook the smile off his face.

The girl made some movements with her hands, which made the boy clap his hands in joy and then he moved his hands in response. Soon they were talking to each other using their hands, facial expressions, and bodies to communicate with each other.

Those who were watching them were amazed at how they seemed to understand each other. "Ah... they are talking with the use of their hands," explained Arnold, as he was the first to recover and understand (which made him first twice more - as he would happily tell anyone who would listen).

Roger, upon seeing the problems as well as the possibilities, suggested, "Well... I propose that that girl and boy should be trained together seeing as they can hand talk and understand each other."

Francis pursed his lips to aid his thoughts, finally saying, "There is a spell that would make the signs they are using into words. Now, how does it go?" He then pulled his face into shapes that proved he had never done so in front of a mirror or he would have worn a bag of some description over his head. Finally he smiled, "Ahh! Right... it is like this." He spoke ancient words as his hands wove the spell towards the two figures that were now deep in conversation.

Suddenly, over the noise of Tom's monologue and the Mountain Boy's dissertation, they watched and listened. They heard the girl ask the boy in bad sign language. "*You deaf in family one*?" Then they heard the words. "Are you the only one who is deaf in your family, or are there others?" This happened because the signs they were using were symbols with a lot more meanings indicated by the body and especially the face.

The spell could only make the signs into words and not interpret them fully. The signs were unlike words or pictures for they did not stand for only one thing but were more of a concept. So while the wizards only heard *"Me, parents hear. Only one deaf in-group, old woman young learn by other deaf people,"* Tara could understand what he was saying as she knew how to speak with her hands: "Both of my parents are hearing. I am the only one in the whole of my group who is totally deaf. I was taught how to use sign language by an old woman who was herself taught it when there used to be many others in our group who were deaf."

Nodding, Tara signed again and the wizards heard *"Ugly place me was, hand tied hit bad. Small places me in. Met three other deaf in little box. No talk except to them so they taught me."* The boy understood this as, "I was a slave in a city that was corrupt and bad. I was kept prisoner in various pens and spent a while with three deaf people who taught me how to sign quite a bit, as they could not understand me so I was forced to learn so that I could communicate with them."

Shaking his head, indicating that he understood what she had told him, he smiled at her then he glanced at the rest of the potentials asking, *"They who?"* "Who are those people?"

*"Us same."* "Same as us I think."

*"Here why?"* "Why are we hear[13]?"

*"Learn same them. Wizards teach us same them."* "To learn magic from the wizards so that one day we can become wizards just like them."

*"Me want learn too, not be me?"* "I would like to become a wizard too, but I can't."

*"Why not?"* "Why not?"

*"Deaf me."* "Because I am deaf and unable to learn."

Tara stood to her full height and, sticking out her chin, pointed to the mountain boy and the boy from the monastery, signing angrily, *"Gone-slave me, filthy dirty that one and him ugly same."* "I am an ex-slave, that boy over there is dirty, and that one is ugly, so what does that mean?" She

---

Not a typo (typed error) but an attempt at humor… I did say attempt.

told him, then she shrugged her shoulders and shook her head. "It means nothing at all."

Then she pointed to the wizards as she signed to the boy, *"They different shapes, and types. We can learn and if they say no then we stay together, right?"* "All of the wizards look and are different from each other but they are still wizards. If they say that we cannot learn from them, then we will stay together, right?"

Happily, the small figure jumped up and down as he signed to her, *"Agreed right, learn and stay if the old wrinkled ones do not want us then stay together."*

Tara slapped him on the shoulder making him take a couple of involuntary steps forward. He frowned from surprise then stepped back so that he could see what she was signing, *"We stay together always always."*

Tara and the small boy laughed loudly, feeling happy that perhaps things would work out all right after all, now that they had a plan. The wizards looked to one another, then they bowed in respect at another way of communicating that worked as well as any of the other ways they knew - and better than a lot of them.

Bill spoke to the assembled wizards who stood (or sat) watching the interchange between Tara and the forest boy. He suggested that as he had found the slave girl then maybe he should be the one who trained her - and that.

Albert looked at him out of the corner of his eye trying to hide the hope from his voice as he asked, "What about the boy? She is the only one who can talk to him."

Shrugging, Bill told him, "I could take him as well... and why not? Two should be as easy as one or as hard, for that matter. Yes, I will enjoy the challenge and it will be good for me - and that."

Albert resisted the urge to rub his hands in glee (glee again! Just where people get all this glee from I would like to know[14]). Instead, he put them out of sight behind his back and held the feelings of release inside until he could enjoy them to their, and his, fullest, later.

Frank turned to Wilfred and asked if he was intending to teach the girl with the strange hair and words that he had brought back, hoping that this would start an argument.

Wilfred looked at the child and then at Frank before saying that he would if no one better wanted to teach her, especially as he liked her spirit and found her language interesting.

"Look at thaaat!"

They all turned to look at Roger and then followed where his finger indicated. It was pointing to the tall girl with yellow hair who had moved determinedly towards Tom, who stood transfixed (this time by his own restraint rather than by magic) as he stared at the tall blonde female farmer moving ever closer to him. When she was just inches away and staring deep into his eyes she asked him, "Are yea intended?"

"N... n... not aver - I mean... naw I ammmmmmm..." The rest of Tom's sentence was smothered by the lips of the girl who encased his thin body with arms of steel, pressing him close to her.

"Well, look at that!" Roger repeated, continuing to point unnecessarily at the couple. Even Jack had opened half of

---

[14] I have been wondering about this and think that there must be some Glee mines somewhere - maybe near the south coast - but how they transport it and in what, is still a mystery to me! As is how and by whom is it distributed?

one eye to witness whatever it was that had caused Roger to be so surprised that he had repeated himself. Douglas, Martin, Wilfred, and Colin laughed aloud at the expression on Frank's face as he complained, "I do not expect to have to witness this kind of thing, and in public as well!"

"Don't be so old fashioned, Frank; I think it's nice and normal."

"It may be normal for you, perhaps, Roger, but not for me... not in any way! That kind of thing is something I was glad to get away from - it shouldn't be allowed!"

"Frank, don't you remember being young and in love?" Roger asked, smiling happily at Frank's discomfort.

We will never know if Frank either did remember being young or in love; for at that point Wilfred asked, "Do you think we should feed them?"

They turned to look at him - then realising that it was simply Wilfred thinking that the young people could be hungry and that he was not actually making a comment about the kissing couple - they then set about invoking a feast for their guests. The wizards spelled tables and tablecloths laden with plates of food and glasses of drinks while Douglas stepped forward and looked at the bunch of dirty old men giving each one a good look as he tried to imagine how the apprentices would see them, but failed.

During the feast, many discussions and conversations jumped and bounced around the long food-filled table. Some of these conversations between the wizards used words and some were in wizard telepathy, whereas some of the dialogue between the wizards and the apprentices was in words. In one case it was held by a wizard watched by a small round spotty face who said nothing as she ate a great deal of food. At the other end of the table Tara acted as an interpreter for Mocker and Bill in between mouthfuls of food and drink.

A small part of these conversations was more a form of gentle inquiry. Harmonisation was the important thing to maintain, Arnold mused; he sent waves of harmony around the table and at the occupants. He knew that discussions and disputes would come later, especially if Frank had anything to do with it!

Albert and Joe ate and smiled to each other. They were very happy to have lost their finds; for, as Joe reasoned, if the girl was going to fall for every boy she saw then she was not the right kind of person to become a wizard. And Albert reasoned that as his find was deaf then it was out of his hands.

Roger watched the potential apprentices as he tried to remember their names. The baby with the red hair had the unusual name of Follia; the multi-haired girl was called... no, he had forgotten (if had ever known it), and the deaf boy was Mocker as the sign spell had informed him. As for the dark-skinned boy, the mountain boy, and the muscle girl, he did not know their names. Jack left the whole process of conversing to his fellow wizards, although he occasionally murmured the odd happy word in his sleep – but to who knows whom... or to who... or what. The other exception to this abundance of words was Tom and the girl with yellow hair whose name turned out to be Myrtle, after her mother's third cousin. This was due mainly to the fact that they sat staring into each other's eyes and holding hands, oblivious to everything and everyone around them. After a few failures to get either of their attention, the wizards gave up and left them to themselves as they concentrated on their other options.

Bill was now talking to the slave girl and the deaf boy; the magic air spell made the boy's signs weave themselves into sound, and made Bill's sounds into signs. It sounded like this (bold type) to any of the wizards who were watching, thanks to the spell, but to the three who were involved it was more like this (italic type). So, Bill's words, "*Show you, and learn pointy hat magic.*" translated to Mocker as, "I will teach you about wizard magic."

Then Mocker signed, "*Yes, want learn lots. How*?" and the spell made it back into words that Bill could understand, "Yes, I really want to learn but how will you teach me?"

"*Show you - you try - until you learn.*" "I will teach you spells, words, things, and you will practice until you learn."

"*Me her*?" "Both her and I together?"

Bill turned to Tara then asked, "*You learn, girl*?" "Do you want to learn wizard magic, girl?"

"*Yes. Want me learn same.*" Tara signed back to him. "Yes, I want to learn as much as I can."

"*I happy you both.*" "I am happy that you both want to learn with me about magic and becoming a wizard."

Each of the wizards who had brought back a potential apprentice tried to answer any questions that they asked. Then they explained that they would teach them what they knew about being a wizard - if the higher council approved them. Those who were not involved like Albert, Colin, Douglas, Jack, Roger, Albert, and Marcus each concentrated on eating their fill without having to bother about talking or even thinking. This task was made all the more interesting to Albert who was still celebrating getting out of training the deaf forest boy.

Bill asked the ex-slave what her name was and whether she wanted to keep it or find a new one. She told him her name was Tara and that she was happy to keep it, as they now knew each other pretty well. Then he asked her where she had learnt to use her hands to talk. The deaf boy watched her lips closely as she explained about the three deaf slaves who had taught her.

Bill asked the boy the same questions; his given name was Quentin but he told them (via the signs) that the other children called him Mocker because he had to copy them to understand what was going on. He said that he would like to have a new name but did not know what yet. Bill nodded, saying that whenever he was ready he could choose one.

Then Bill asked them if they would teach him how to hand talk without magic - and that. Tara hid her surprise and turned to face Mocker, trying to tell him that he was a better signer so it should be him doing the teaching. The boy watched her hands as she repeated this in sign until he opened his eyes wide in utter amazement and disbelief. He kept on looking from one to the other until he was sure that it was not a joke. Then he nodded and grinned as he smiled at them both, shaking his head. Mocker could not believe that any grown up, let alone someone as grand as a wizard, would want to learn sign language - and that even if they did then they wouldn't want him to teach them. Feeling the happiest he had ever felt in his entire life, he started the old wizard's training immediately by showing him that the vowels were the thumb and fingers of one hand before Bill could change his mind.

Reginald helped himself to choice morsels as he

repeatedly told his charge that it was all right to eat and that he was a wizard and not a god; and that he should not keep on debasing himself as it was unnecessary and besides it got in the way of eating.

Martin helped the chubby child to hold her food and drink without dropping too much of it. He kept on smiling at her as he told her that everything would be all right from now on, that no one would bully her while he was around and that he would do whatever he could for her. She watched him with her wide open eyes but said nothing.

Wilfred sat opposite the girl who was saying, "Gift of wiz is cherry but goops in a hole is dark side with the lid down." Wilfred translated her words into (A chance to become a wizard is a wonderful opportunity but the other apprentices look inferior to the task and not worth my time or effort to get to know them.)

Nodding his understanding, he replied in his best kid-speak. "Dooks look dim but time giver learn-space with sound-flow get top filled with control pack." He mentally translated what he hoped he had told her into (Give them time and when they start to learn things and gain knowledge they may obtain control of themselves and start to understand and become nice people.) They both then fell silent, nodding and looking around at the goops and dooks that wandered around them in stick taste. (Inferior beings that seemed not to be taking responsibility for being there).

Henry discovered that the boy he removed from outside the monastery was called Keryon, who now informed him that he was keen to give wizardry a go, as he did not have much else on presently, but only if they treated him right.

While the trainers were conversing with their charges,

the council finished their meal and moved away so that they could have their own discussion.

Frank was saying. "On further consideration, I have come to the conclusion that having females will cause even more problems than I first thought they would. Look at Tom and... what's her name... as an example." He glanced at Tom and Myrtle who were sitting, holding hands and staring into each other's eyes.

"I think it is nice," Arnold said, smiling, making him look like a pumpkin with a wrinkled curved slash.

"Arnold - you are going soft in your old age."

"Roger - I am not old but I am a little soft, but I was the first let me remind you once again!"

To stop Arnold and Roger going into one of their silly discussions Douglas asked, "Frank, man, what is your problem as yee see it?"

"Thank you, Douglas. There are so many - where shall I begin?"

"I suggest the usual place, Frank - at the beginning," Arnold suggested happily.

Frank shook his head and waved his hands around, threatening to dislodge his hat as he explained. "I was not asking. It was a rhetorical question."

Arnold smiled and folded his hands across his chest as he observed, "Have you noticed that you don't get as many of those as you used to?"

Trying to ignore him, Frank shook his shoulders, saying, "As I was saying, Arnold. There are so many problems. Where will they sleep for one thing? And how will we be able to keep them from becoming soppy? It is only a question of time until something bad happens to them or they do something. They might run away - or worse, disobey us." He shivered at the idea of having someone else disagreeing with him.

Francis scratched his ear, avoiding Frank's eye as he said, "They can leave at any time, as can any of us. That is not a problem. Could we not give them two sleeping places, one for the males and one for the females? That would not be too hard, would it Colin?"

"No, that's an easy spell," Colin replied, grinning happily at Frank who shook his robe as he told them, "It will only be a question of time before it goes bad, you will see."

"Are those your only concerns, Frank?" Roger asked, sensing that there was more to Frank's concerns other than the obvious.

"You need more?" Frank asked him, making his fingers into a sort of a roof as he pointed out with his chin what to him was obvious. "Very well. How about the fact that female energy leaks?"

"Technically, it doesn't leak but flows out and allows other energies to enter."

Frank gave Francis a superior look as he replied. "You are splitting hairs, Francis."

"How do you do that again?" Arnold asked, hiding his amusement.

Roger grinned as he replied, "That is an easy question - you have to use a small sharp axe, of course."

"Don't you mean a *very* small one to hit the hair on the back of its neck?"

"Arnold, dear boy, I am sure that Francis is talking about hares, not hairs."

"How do you know he is talking about hares?"

"Look, it is now me who is saying the saying, so I know what I mean. I mean 'splitting hares'."

"If you say so, but which did Francis mean and which one did Frank mean?"

Ignoring the attempt to get him involved in one of their silly word games, Francis pointed out, "We are moving away from Frank's point; what can we do about the difference in their personal energy fields?"

"When you say field..."

"Stop it, Arnold! Francis is asking about female energy flow as well you know."

"There's nay ways for us ta block 'em I suppose?" Douglas suggested, trying to keep the discussion this side of silliness.

"Possibly, Douglas," said Francis, "but if we did, then they would not be technically female anymore."

Hiding his grin, Arnold pointed out, "You do use technically quite a lot, Francis."

Francis missed the motivation behind Arnold's words as he became involved in one of his favourite subjects, the meaning of words. He tilted his head to one side as he started to explain, "I think that the word 'technically' explains my thoughts better than any other I can think of. I could of course use procedure, or process, or technique, manner, way, or even method - but I prefer to use 'technically' as I like it the most. It describes the objective possibility of the subject using just a hint of science. Yes that is definitely the reason why I use…" He glanced at Arnold who had covered his mouth as he laughed silently behind it. "Oh brother! You got me caught up in your silly game."

"Let us get back to the point," suggested Roger with a

smile, "So, if we interfere or change their energy fields, then they won't be female, am I right?"

"That is so," replied Francis, watching Arnold who was still trying not to laugh aloud.

"Then that solves our problem! Let's do it at once," Frank said, clapping his hands together and rolling his shoulders.

"But Frank - that would be unfair - and probably not nice into the bargain if we were to alter their gender." Arnold looked at Frank as he suggested, "Perhaps we should try it on one of us first? How about you, Frank?"

Frank spluttered at the suggestion, shaking his head and dislodging his hat.

"If it works then why not do it?" said Francis, as Colin held his sides as his laughter bubbled up in him as Roger asked, "How would you go about it anyway?"

"Roger, don't you mean how would *we* go about it - if we decided to go about it - which technically we have not yet decided to do?"

Francis was tapping his chin and pursing his lips to aid his thoughts until he replied, "It would mean that most of the work would fall on the shoulders of those who were doing the training."

"That is the way it always ees?"

"You are right, Douglas. What do you say, Francis?"

"Thank you, Arnold. I have no historic records to help me, so I am on my own."

"No you are not... we are all here."

"Stop it, Roger! That is not funny."

"It's better than your splitting hair thing..."

Francis held up his hands, then gave them the wisdom of his brief contemplation; "I think that a female has an energy field like that for a reason. I think that we should not interfere with it as it would be an infringement of the individual's right and the results could be very hard for them to live with. I do think that we should progress to teach them in the normal way, if only in the name of science, and realising that there could be a risk somewhere to someone or something along the way. I still say that we should try to teach them as they are."

Douglas and Albert agreed, while Colin waved his hand meaning that he just wanted them to keep on talking as he was having so much fun. Frank shook his head at Colin who smiled back, then started to giggle again.

Ignoring him, Frank said, "So we should get rid of them as I said in the first place."

"Frank, don't you remember? It was I who was in first place."

"Arnold," scoffed Roger, "that is really bad."

"Thank you, Roger, I thought so. So what shall we do about it, and especially with them?" He pointed to where Tom and Myrtle still sat holding hands and gazing into each other's eyes.

"We can send them all back and make them as they were. They should never have been brought here in the first place."

"Frank, really! If they fall in love then we must allow them to do so. It is nature - and you know what happens when we interfere with nature?"

Frank opened his eyes at the memory of his early experiments with nature that he thought only he and his teacher had known about.

Before Arnold could respond, Roger came to Frank's rescue, saying, "As far back as I have knowledge of, wizards have never married - let alone fallen in love."

"What about Marcus?" Colin pointed to the small figure of Marcus who was still trying to be as small as possible. Looking at Marcus, Roger said, "Well, he is the exception that proves the rule. Anyway he was married a long time ago."

"Is there a rule or something that says wizards cannot get married?" asked Arnold, wanting to know the answer.

Frowning and rocking on his heels, Francis told them, "There do not seem to be any rules as such about females becoming wizards or of wizards not being able to marry; nothing on the subject as far as I have had the time to research into the matter. Wizards on the whole seem to be satisfied with wizardry alone but I have come across a few way back in history who married but cannot find any females as such who became wizards."

"So what did they marry, then?"

Francis raised his eyebrows until he realised what he had said. "I meant that there have not been any female wizards that I could find, not that they have not married any females, as you well know."

They smiled at him until Arnold said, "Anyway Frank, suppose that they do all fall in love with each other, what then?" He asked this as innocently as he could.

It was left to Francis to put into words, "Wizards falling in love with wizards?" Colin observed what an interesting chapter of research that would make, and wondered how many times this had already happened.

"No, it is not right. Apprentices falling in love with apprentices? It is disgusting and wrong," replied Frank, the irritation plainly showing in his voice.

Francis cleared his throat in preparation to reveal a few known cases of wizard love; but he suddenly thought better of it so said nothing.

Colin, who had managed to control his mirth, pointed out, "They are not yet, technically speaking, apprentices - only people who have been brought here to see if they could become so."

Frank glared at Colin, who started to laugh again, making Frank wave his hands around saying that they all would fall in love with each other and that it would cause the end of them all.

"Why are you so keen on finding problems, Frank?" Roger asked him gently.

"I am not. I am just trying to keep this situation sane. Females have never been wizards and should never become wizards. It will diminish our magic; bringing in inferior females with their second-rate ways."

Francis scratched his neck, then said; "I can't find any reason in the books why females cannot learn wizardry. The only energy difference was noted along with animal and plant energy by way of explaining the differences, while hermaphrodites have a completely different one that explains that they are incompatible with either of the other types.

"I can see no reason why females could not learn to use both kinds of energy and manage to incorporate them. And in no way do any of my books suggest that one way of learning or of using energy control is superior to another."

"There you go then, that is enough," said Arnold.

Moving closer until he was standing over the small man, Frank stared down as he told him, "Arnold, we are nowhere.

So what happens if we try to teach them spells and the magic spills out of them? It might even harm them," he added, hoping that he would be there to watch when it did.

Smiling and making his face look even more skull-like, Francis replied, "I am glad that you are thinking of them as people, Frank. I have said there is no written knowledge in any of my books on the subject that I know about. I think that maybe it has never happened before so we do not know of any outcome; but if we go slowly and carefully then who knows what the result will be? If we encounter problems then we will either be able to solve them or stop the... ah... experiment."

They all looked at the tall wizard considering his words until Colin said, "Maybe they will be even better than men *because* of the differences."

Each wizard showed surprise in their own way at this; Arnold gasped, Frank spluttered, Jack slept, Albert coughed in shock, Douglas threw his head to one side and thought about the possibility while Joe ignored it (and them). Francis opened his eyes to their fullest, rubbed his chin, and shook his head in dismay.

Frank was the first to recover, saying, "Colin, that is preposterous!"

Becoming even more serious[15], Colin replied, "Why is it, Frank? Just because it has never happened before does not mean that it should never happen. Maybe the reason why it hasn't is because no one has ever thought of it before or they have only seen it as a threat rather than a possibility."

---

[15] So how could Colin become more serious? He either was serious or he was not. Well, Colin was a wizard and wizards can become a lot more (and a lot less) of most things than we can.

Roger wobbled forward, saying, "I agree with Colin. Maybe way back when the world was full of wizards, magicians, wiccans, witches, wise women, and the like, the men kept women out because they could have become better wizards than they were."

"That is absolute nonsense, complete, and utter nonsense in every way!" Frank said, folding his arms and trying to look superior.

"That observation is not based on anything other than your personal feelings, Frank. Or is it?" Arnold asked, feeling happy at Frank's discomfort as he replied, "It is complete rubbish; even you must draw the line somewhere."

"I take that as a 'no' then?" Roger asked, half-smiling; he was keeping the other half of the smile to use on Arnold later on.

"Roger, will you please give him some space to squirm." Arnold asked happily.

"Anything you say, Arnold." replied Roger with a fat smile.

"Frank, there is no way we can know if a female can adapt to our way of using magic without allowing them to try," Francis pointed out (much to Arnold's frustration for he had wanted to point out that point).

"That does seem ta make sense," said Douglas.

Then Colin said, "I agree, Douglas, and I think that we should try it. As an experiment it would make an interesting entry in our history books if nothing else."

Francis contemplated the idea and as he rubbed his chin, he mentally started to write the heading of the chapter on the first female wizards.

"Thee are only people after all," said Douglas. "We ken

just experiment on theem as if they were jeest things."

Arnold gave Douglas a glaring stare (which is more fun to say than to write by the way) as he said, "But, Douglas, dear fellow, we are wizards and we have always used people to experiment on. We also experiment on ourselves and everything else all the time." He looked at Frank as he continued, "And some of us think that is what people are there for... that, and to get in our way...."

"That is true, yes," Roger replied, looking around at the other wizards through half-closed eyes.

Starting to get bored and wanting to examine the candidates, Colin asked, "So how do we vote?"

Nodding his agreement to show that he also thought it was time to vote, Arnold asked, "Is Jack awake?"

"How can you tell?" Albert asked, studying the small wrinkled figure that looked like it had been carved from mushrooms. Roger glanced down at Jack for a moment, then announced, "He is asleep - but that probably won't stop him voting."

"As the first, I say that we give them a chance to at least start training as apprentices," Arnold said as importantly as he could.

"I have to agree with Arnold," said Roger, then looking over at Frank said, "Frank?"

Shaking his head, Frank told them, "I think it will all end in tears. I say send them all back before it is too late. If we do not then we are all doomed."

Colin voted for them to stay and have a chance, as did Douglas. "We are all in agreement except for Frank... oops, sorry Jack," Roger apologised to the inclining figure that had now opened one of his eyes - the left one this time.

Straining his voice to be heard above those of the feast takers, the oldest member gave them the wisdom of his sleepy thinking. “I say give them a chance, but will we have to tell them that it is all new? or what... or... what?” Jack slid back into sleep leaving the rest of the council with a couple of problems; that of understanding what he had just said and then what to do about what he had just said once they had finally understood it. Eventually they realised that Jack had asked whether they should tell the female apprentices that they might be the first females to learn wizardry, or should they not.

“So, we all agree to give them a chance, except for Frank. That then is carried, we will give them a chance - but what about what Jack just pointed out?”

“We should tell ’em no more then they needed ta knoo,” said Douglas.

“So do they need to know anything?” Roger asked, looking down at Jack who was smiling in his sleep.

“I would want to know.”

“Yes, but you are just nosey,” Frank told Arnold.

“And you aren’t?” Arnold replied, giving Frank a wrinkled smile.

“Gentlemen!... We must decide before our guests finish their meal,” Roger reminded the rest of the council as well as himself.

Arnold nodded, then said, “I would be the first to say that they should be given the chance but how much we tell them about this being the first time female thing must be up to the individual teachers who will get to know them the best... I was the first here as well by the way.”

“I think that I would want to know each applicant better

before deciding such a thing on their behalf - and only then would I prefer not to have to make the decision until I see if they can learn anything at all," said Francis.

There was a pause as they all turned to look at the tall, thin wizard until Arnold told him, "Francis, you old person you, that is sitting on the fence! But don't worry for I am not going to take it away."

"Take offence... O fence... O no," said Colin, shaking his head in dismay. He gave a lone groan slowly followed by a larger collective one as the rest of the wizards finally got it.

"No Arnold, I mean what I say," Francis told him, ignoring the play on words, "Once they have been told, then only a spell could stop them knowing it and the knowledge could affect, well must affect, how they behave. But then, if you tell one then they will want to tell the others; and if you do not tell them, then when they do find out they might have a big problem with us for not telling them in the first place. My history books are of no help on this subject, it is up to us."

Colin, on seeing that some of the recruits were getting tired and his chance to study them that day was slipping away, said, "So, can we vote on the matter?"

Douglas spoke next, saying, "Maybe we should let people know that we is not deed - theen maybe we wouldnae be having a problem of finding apprentices - an then we wouldnae have ta consider females."

Frank moved forward, glad to be able to insert his presence once more. "Douglas, if people knew about us, then they would be all over the place asking stupid questions and asking us to do things for them, horrible!"

"Don't worry, Frank - any normal person who sees you

would not be brave enough to try to bother you, especially if you were wearing your hat."

"Leave my hat out of this, Arnold, will you?" Frank retorted angrily.

"It is so large that ignoring it is going to be a problem, but I will try to ignore it even if it does dominate somewhat." Arnold replied, grinning happily.

Shaking his head and his fists, Frank demanded of them, "So are you going ahead with this training with them, or not?"

Roger shrugged, saying, "We are, Frank. Perhaps one of us should always be available - to make sure that the apprentices change their clothes and wash occasionally and eat properly and to learn how to get on with others?"

"I was never taught how to get on with people."

"Oh really, Arnold, were you not?"

"So, who taught you so badly, Roger?"

"That is not very nice now, Arnold, is it?"

Before Arnold could reply, saying that he was getting tired, Frank told them, "In the old days a wizard looked after his own apprentice as they travelled across the land."

"Who wants to travel anywhere anymore, Frank? And anyway what if you had a female apprentice?"

Frank shuddered at the thought, as Arnold said, "Not me for one! I like the way we used to do it, each of us teach them something, and then pass them on to someone else."

Colin spoke next, watching Frank from the corner of his eye as he gave his views thus, "I think that we should let each apprentice have mainly one wizard to train them. In that way if there is any contamination it will only affect one person and the rest of us will be safe."

All were in favour except for Frank and Joe (who had joined them as he was getting bored with the meal and with waiting for them to finish).

"We should send them back before there is trouble," said Joe. Frank clapped his hands together, muttering that at last someone was talking sense. Douglas reminded them that Joe was not on the inner council, only on the outer one. Joe sniffed and pulled his lips down as Douglas adjusted his glasses saying, "Joe n Frank, we huv voted ta give theem a chance ta accept it, soo can we get on?"

"Having females around will change our way of life and who knows? It could be the end of us! And who knows what the consequences will be to the entire world?"

Roger smiled at Frank as he said, "Frank, you do look on the dark side. Maybe it will be the beginning of us, how about that?"

Francis nodded and pointed out that they had no way of knowing what the consequences of their actions would be.

"Not everything is black and white," added Arnold, sneering at Frank in a friendly way.

Colin saw the look of anger that passed over Frank's face, so he turned to Arnold and Roger and told them, "You two are so flash!"

"That is a bright idea?" Arnold responded, grinning happily.

"Gentlemen... enough... please?" Francis asked, then continued, "As far as I am concerned we have no way of knowing what will happen as we appear to be the first wizards to try to teach females as far back as records began. As we are already breaking with tradition, then why not go all the way? What we are doing here is writing history."

Francis nodded and clapped his hands in sheer enjoyment as he carried on, "Of course we do this all the time, but it is all a matter of degrees." They all looked at him as if he had told them the sun is up in the sky so he asked them. "I agree that what we are doing is new and that is fine, but do we keep quiet about the energy difference or do we think they need to know to help their training? Roger, what do you say?"

"Tell them if it would be best, but it should depend on each person - and they shouldn't tell anyone else."

"Francis?"

"Go all of the way and tell them if they are ready to understand but only if they are ready."

"Ah, Albert - what do you say about the new recruits?"

"I think we should tell them to go away."

"Actually we have already voted to let them stay to see what is possible. So, they are to be taught - do you have anything else to add?"

Albert bowed his head and studied the ground, feeling too foolish to say anything else.

Instead, Arnold said, "Tell them nothing. Let them find out when they are using magic as with the rest of magic learning."

"Douglas?"

"Say naught ta theem, let 'em work it oot if they can."

"Joe?"

"Give it a try already as you have already voted on it."
"Frank, do you have anything else to add?"

Glancing at Albert and Joe, he said, "Only that it will all end in tears - or much worse - and much, much worse than any nightmare."

Arnold started to say that Frank had too much 'much' in his life but before he got the words out, Roger told them, "I say tell them if they are ready to know, but only when they are able to understand the implications of the matter in its fullest meaning. How much we tell them now must be down to each trainer as they will have to take full responsibility for them, what they know, how much information they are given, and how it may affect them and any other people around them. On how much they are ready to receive must also be a personal judgment on the teacher or trainer's part. However much that may be, I advise that this information is not passed on to any of them who may not be ready to receive the same amount as each other or anything under the same level of knowledge as this could slant their training."

Roger glanced at Arnold who was frowning with his head to one side then grinning he continued, "Now, how much each should be told (if any) - and only then if it can be contained and not passed on - seems to be the problem. This must mean in any form or amount of what they (the teller) knows, they must not tell anyone who would not be capable of understanding the information or indeed of telling others even if some of the others already know. This will also include them and even if they are ready or not to know or unable not to pass on any, I said any, of the information to others who may or may not be ready to receive such information...."

Roger tried to untwist his mind, which had been trying to follow Arnold's words too closely and was now paying the price. Frank went off in a huff (well it was more like a dark cloud of smoke, but it had the same sound and effect as a huff). Jack woke up and opened all of one eye (his left). It had a question in it which Roger answered, "We have voted to give the girls a chance to know about them being the first, to be taught only when they are able and ready to understand, but we will have to put an inhibitor on them not to tell anyone who is not ready."

"Frank has gone off because he does not agree with us - he wants to send them back," added Arnold.

Jack blinked then slowly closed his left eye and soon both eyes had joined the rest of him in deep slumber.

Roger scratched his ear. "Do you think that Frank will be all right?" he asked Arnold.

"He never was before, so why should he be now?"

"You are right again and that makes three times today."

"Four times... and I was the first."

Francis left Arnold and Roger to argue and eagerly went to his newest history book where he immediately started to write: *The council sat to discuss the problem of how much knowledge should be given to the apprentices about their unique status......"*

Albert moved over to where Marcus stood and slapped him on the back saying, "We are all right. It looks as if the two we brought will want to stay together with any luck." He indicated Tom and Myrtle, who still sat holding hands unaware of anything but each other. Then they glanced across at Mocker who sat signing with Bill and Tara. They had lost their apprentices and could go back to what they had been doing before. Marcus kept quiet, as he was not sure that he had tried hard enough with Tom; and even though he did not really want to get involved in training anyone, he was feeling a little guilty about what he had or had not done.

# Chapter Fourteen: Apprentice Time

Those wizards who were going to do the main training of an apprentice (or apprentices in Bill's case) set about invoking two large cabins, one for the boys and one for the girls. Each was completed with enough beds, glasses of water, boring and interesting books and the odd teddy bear so that all the children got a good night's rest. This only happened after the wizards had cajoled the young ones into bed, got the others tired and finally put a sleep spell over both buildings that would last until they undid it.

In this way, everyone had a good night's sleep - except for Francis who spent most of the night writing up the latest four chapters of *The Wizards of Pearland* with the sub heading of "Obtaining an apprentice." He described each applicant, both physically and energetically, then went on to write about their actions until it came to Mocker, where he described the use of the hands, body, and especially the face to replace language. He had read many books on the subject and used various spells to fill in any gaps until he felt that he was sufficiently qualified to describe the process, if nothing else. His report on the higher council meeting and what had been said left a little to be desired for he left out anything that he saw as not necessary, silly, unobtrusive, misleading or not very wizardly – needless to say, most of what was left was boring!

The next morning, after the wizards had produced

breakfasts for themselves and the children, each wizard moved away with his apprentice (or apprentices in Bill's case) to start their new lives.

Martin walked slowly, very slowly indeed... no, even slower than that... because he had to walk at the pace of the small, chubby red-haired Follia. She had eaten little but she had drunk a great deal, and so far she had spoken only the odd word. From these three facts that had emerged, it was the last one that worried Martin the most. In a soft, kind voice he asked her, "So my dear, how are you?"

She stopped walking and looked up into his face and he noticed that she was breathing heavily as she told him, "Good, happy."

He smiled, wondering how he was going to explain to her the fundamentals of self-awareness and basic magic, let alone teach her how to say spells in ancient languages when she could not even string a full sentence together. They walked a little further until she sat down on the dry ground like an old dog and stared up at him as if he was her mother. Tilting his head to one side he asked, "Do you like trees or fields or sea or lakes or mountains or... what sort of areas do you like?"

She furrowed her brow for a second, then asked what a lake was.

Hiding his shock, he replied that he would show her.

Next minute, the girl was looking at a vast amount of water that looked to her like a million wells all squashed together that had appeared in front of them. She looked at him for permission to investigate and he smiled and waved his hand, giving it, so they ambled closer to the inviting water. He pulled up his robe and tucked it into his belt, then helped her take off her shoes and socks before leading her into the quiet grey-blue water. As she giggled and splashed, he kept the fish and slimy things away from her so that her experience would be as good as he could make it.

Then he told her that there were many such things like this in the land and to get to them all she had to do was think about them as hard as she could. The small, fat form ceased her movements exploring the wonderful feeling of walking in wet mud, and again studied his face looking for a lie; seeing none, she closed her eyes and imagined trees. She heard his encouraging words as she continued with her self-imposed task to remember the few trees she had seen.

"That's the way, little lady - just fill your head with the picture. Make them as real as you can... that's the way," he told her encouragingly, and when she opened her eyes she saw the tall trees of her imagination standing in front of her.

The lake had vanished, leaving a forest in its place. She moved slowly towards the trees until she could put her hands on the rough bark to prove that they were indeed real, and not like the pictures in the books she had seen them in. She turned to look up at him, her face forming a question.

"No, you did not do it all by yourself, but you did some of it. You made the picture very real and I did the rest with magic and spells." He painted a picture in her mind of a happy book with words dancing around. He told her that was where spells came from but explained, "That is how you start: imagine, magnify, and finally manifest. We call it the three M's." He knew even as he spoke that the joke would be lost on her. He smiled as he remembered the first time he had heard it.

Pulling himself back to the now, he looked at his charge

who sat studying a stone she had picked up. The afternoon sun brought out many beautiful shades of red in her hair as she suddenly hugged the stone to her face from sheer pleasure. Martin stroked his chin and smiled down at her, thinking that she had imagination and when she learned to trust, talk, and walk; she might be able to go far.

Not far away, in wizards's terms (which are sharper and a lot thicker but much more pliable than most people's normally are), sat Bill. He was with Tara and Mocker, sitting under the shade of a tree. He slowly used the index finger of his right hand to point to various places and fingers on and around his left hand as he quietly repeated:

A.- B. - C. - D. - E. - F. - G. - H. - I. - J. – K.

Mocker watched as, for the first time in his life, he had become a teacher. Grinning, he waved his hand to get Bill's attention, then showed him where he had gone wrong.

Bill watched and listened to the explanation that Mocker and Tara gave, and then said slowly, "I remember... I think. 'J' is that, 'K' is that, a bit awkward that one - and that. What is next - and that?... Oh, I know 'L' is one finger on the palm; 'M' is three fingers flat pressed onto it. 'N' is two, 'O' is the third finger of the receiving hand and is another one of the vowels."

Mocker touched his arm to get his attention, then showed him that he was wrong again.

"Oh of course, I have mixed up the vowels. 'O' is not the third finger for you start with the thumb, which is the letter, 'A' then 'E' then 'I' and then 'O', so 'O' is the fourth finger. Then we have 'P', 'Q' move it around there to the palm, and we have 'R' then 'S' is the two little fingers linked. 'T' is pointing to the palm where the pad thing divides. 'U' is the little finger and the last vowel. 'V' is two fingers flat on palm; 'W' all fingers crossed. 'X' cross fingers. 'Y' turn receiving hand until fingers and thumb are in front of you and use the index finger of the pointing hand to make a tail thus producing 'Y', then straight fingers into palm of receiving hand making the letter 'Z.'

All three of them clapped their hands and laughed happily at his success on finally getting through the letters of the alphabet. Bill told Mocker that maybe he should change his name and after Tara had interpreted his words, the boy and Tara frowned at him until he explained that as he was now mocking mocker then perhaps he should be Mocking Mocker - and that. They all laughed at his silliness and then Mocker signed that he liked the name Mocker and would keep it as it worked well both ways now. Again they laughed, and then Bill spelled ice cream for them all, making them even happier.

Reginald, however, was not quite as happy as he tried to inform his apprentice that there was no need to fall on his knees every time he did anything for him. He was saying (for the ninth time that morning) "Er... young man... I think that I have mentioned to you that if you carry on... er... doing that you will damage your legs. I am just trying to show you how to begin the... er... um... wizard's way of doing things."

The fair hair waved around the head that moved up and down in supplication as the owner of both of them said, "Ye are wondrous to take the trouble with one who is so not worthy and is lower than a maggot. I swear that I will give you my life in service of thy many kindnesses."

Tutting, Reginald suggested that they could stop for a snack if he was hungry.

The boy replied, "I really am not worth your time - but if you were to throw me a morsel from your table of splendidness then I would crawl across the dirt to accept such a gift from one as kind and magical as thee."

Waving his hand in dismissal, Reginald said, "Whatever" and then spelled another table with its usual (usual for him that is) vast amount of food and drink on it. He stopped and looked at it in admiration then told the boy to help himself but to do so without the usual praising of his wonderfulness and the like, "Umm, just eat and enjoy knowing that you are as... er... um, worthy as the next one. Well, and... er... and a lot better than a lot of the ones after them, I am sure."

The boy bowed and tried to lie on the ground in supplication while reaching for a cake at the same time. He failed, and knocked the cake onto the floor. Reginald sighed heavily, wondering if this boy would ever start to see him as just a man who knew a few things and who did not need or want this constant praising. He took another cake as he watched the hand of his apprentice reach up and tip over a glass of apple juice. Reginald sighed heavily and shook his head, wondering how this would end.

Wilfred smiled at Gloria who was walking from tree to tree, touching them lightly with her fingertips to prove that they were real. Eventually she came and stood before him and asked if he was going to help her to top up. He replied that he was more than willing to help her learn but was unsure as to the best way to go forward.

She folded her thin arms around her thin body and shook her multi-coloured hair as she observed, "Size for one is not for next, so choose a close fitting." (Everybody is different so you do not have to keep to any particular method of teaching, so choose the one that is best for me). He nodded, agreeing that probably the best place to start would be to consider how she would respond the best and to adjust his teaching as they went along.

In another part of the forest, Henry looked at the dark-skinned and even darker-haired boy who was frowning at the area spelled before him. "Do you not like the scenery?" Henry asked.

Through a scowl the boy said, "It's not bad - but I would like more space."

Henry flicked his fingers and the trees thinned out until they found themselves standing in a more open area. Keryon glanced around, then complained that the sun was in his eyes.

Over the next two days, things slowly got worse with the apprentices - for whenever they came together it turned into a major problem for all of them.

The mountain boy could fight better than Keryon and tried to prove it at every opportunity. Follia could only talk and walk a little way but in spite of this, she kept on telling the older ones what to do. Tara and Mocker spent a lot of time together talking with their hands and this annoyed the mountain boy and Gloria. Tara kept the mountain boy from whacking Mocker as easily as he had the monastery boy. On one occasion he had hit Mocker, felt a tap on his shoulder, looked around and - wham! - was knocked off his feet. He shook his head and looked up at Tara who was standing over him, indicating that she wanted him to get up so that she could knock him down again. He had told her that he did not fight girls to which Tara replied that only made her job of knocking him down even easier.

He looked into her eyes and saw that she meant it so told her that he would not hit her 'deafie' again. She nodded then left him and, true to his word, he ignored Mocker completely. Tara and Gloria wouldn't speak, as Tara thought Gloria was looking down on her by using kid-speak and so she spent a lot of time glaring at Gloria.

Gloria (the girl with the multi-coloured hair that swirled around her head every time she moved) would not talk to Follia, Keryon, or Mocker. She thought one was too young, the other a dook, and the last she did not know how to. As she would only speak in her kid-speak, any understanding as to what she was saying took such a lot of hard work on their behalf that most of the others did not bother trying to speak to her.

Soon, Keryon and Gloria took to arguing and trying to shout each other down, much to the annoyance of everyone else who then joined in. The exception to this was Mocker, who sat watching everyone screaming at each other with his head on one side, trying to make out what the words they were throwing at each other meant.

Tom and Myrtle thought only of each other and farms (in that order) and had to be spelled apart otherwise. They would not eat when they were alone and they ignored all the arguments, along with everything else that was not each other.

The two large wooden buildings where the boys and girls slept peacefully did their job and kept their occupants out of trouble, but only after heavy sleep-spells. During the day, when they were all together, it was a total disaster - and getting even worse.

Sunday morning found Reginald walking along with the

boy from the mountain at his side. He was explaining, "Magic, as I... er...have said can be... um... dangerous stuff. It has to be worked with... er... respect and each spell has to be said exactly the way it... um... has been taught and written." He looked at the boy who was staring at him with his usual wide-eyed devotion. Reginald shook his head, then tried again, "...Er... and they have to be remembered word for word, as they have... er... been handed down to us and if they are not said exactly then things can go badly wrong. Yes, very badly wrong."

The boy nodded, then replied in his usual exaggerated way, "Thou are wonderful to give one such as I, being unworthy, the time to learn gifts of magic. I will be thy slave and will do anything you ask, just command me and you will see that I a..."

Reginald flicked his fingers and the boy lost the power of anything - especially speech - and stood gaping up at him. Looking deep into the staring eyes, the old man said, "Dear boy, please just try to say what you... er... say in a shortened form please. Now... umm, are you hungry?" Without waiting for an indication of agreement, he manifested a small table with the usual large amounts of food and drink on it.

When the boy could, he proclaimed that he was indeed a master of the occult and the finest of all of those who wielded magic, until a look from Reginald finally succeeded in shutting him up. Chewing slowly, the wizard studied the young man who was now clean and dressed in a garment he had chosen from the thirty-three Reginald had offered him. It hung around him as if he were a scarecrow. His cuts and bruises had now healed and apart from fighting with the other apprentices, he did everything he was told. He did nothing of his own accord (except for arguing and fighting with the other apprentices) so when Reginald tried to show him something, the boy just told him how wonderful he was instead of trying to copy or learn from him. He never asked any questions, only repeated his praise of the wizard and to say how unworthy he was to have been accepted into his company.

After the meal, Reginald scratched his head considering his choices, then chanted a spell that showed him the boy's mental makeup. Instantly he saw the swirling mass that made up the boy's identity, and slowly he read that the boy would never be at his best working alone unless something forced him to change. He needed someone or something to work for, someone he could keep above him, and this would go on until something made him take responsibility for his being alive. He would work tirelessly for this person or deity, as he thought that was all he was good enough for - again until something happened to change him.

Reginald thought of the many ways that he could make him change. But to change him with spells or magic would mean changing him beyond all recognition of what he could be. It would be wrong to reform him or shock him into accepting that he was as good as anyone else was, he had to find that out for himself. Deciding that forcing change on him was not a decent thing to do, Reginald considered how this personality could fit into wizardry. No matter how hard he tried to picture him as a wizard it did not fit, and he realised the boy would never be happy trying to do something that he did not want to do.

Nodding to himself and spelling another cake, he

continued to consider. He could not see the boy changing and he did not see how he could teach him anything until he did. The boy usually ate little as he watched the wizard's every move so that he could do the right thing to please him. Finally, Reginald came to a decision and smiled broadly for two reasons. Firstly because it would not involve asking anyone else and secondly because it would help both him and the boy. Then he folded his hands in his lap saying, "Umm... er... which of all the gods do you... er... think is the mightiest of them... um... all?"

Bowing and keeping his head lowered, the boy replied in a hushed voice, "The mightiest and truest of all of the great gods must be that of the great sky god Dia. Long is his arm and wise is her wisdom, going beyond the understanding of all but a few enlightened blessed ones. I am a better person just for saying his name. May we all become worthy of his wisdom before we all become dust under her sandals?"

Wondering why a god would bother to wear sandals, Reginald asked his companion if he had ever considered becoming a priest.

The response was not quite what he expected, for the boy threw himself onto the ground and started to hit his head crying, "Priest! Priest! Me a priest? I come from the mountain range of Walleye and it is a sin to think that anyone from there could ever be more than a temple hawker - and that only after generations of study. If the gods are willing, then in my next life I may be worthy to start on the road to devotion. I am theirs to do with as they may, any sacrifice, for sacrifice is all that I am worth." With the last sentence, he threw out his arms and legs then squashed his head into the dirt and lay splayed like some form of squashed starfish.

Sighing, Reginald asked, "Now then, just say that I... er... could arrange for you to be taken on as a trainee priest, umm... would that be worthy for you to... um... do?"

The boy lifted his head showing the tears that poured from his eyes as he again repeated that he was not worthy.

Reginald frowned to help him get his bearings and then disappeared to find a priest.

When he next appeared some time later, the boy seemed not to have moved, but he noticed that there were fewer cakes than before. So smiling, Reginald helped him to his feet, then ate another cake before spelling them both to meet the priest who would be his new teacher.

It had been an easy task to find a priest of Dia who would accept a disciple being offered by a wizard, especially one that was offering a large sum of money. He took the boy and introduced him to the priest.

Before he could leave, the boy knelt before him with lots of "Thou art the finest and closest to the hand of god and I am unworthy to hold the memory of our meeting in a mind as unformed and unholy as mine." Then some, "Wondrous the day when wizards were allowed to walk the earth and to talk to unworthiness such as…"

Reginald read the energy of the priest and wondered how long he would put up with one such as this boy. Then he thought, "hey! He's got me at it now, talking longer than is needed, and... er, using odd words. Now, I must stop this." Finally, after saying his goodbyes to the priest and the boy, he spelled himself back to the quiet, comfortable forest where he had been trying to teach the boy and had a small, peaceful meal by way of celebration.

Later, Reginald explained to the council what he had done. Some of them were a little surprised at him being so forthright in making a decision and then acting on it without asking beforehand. But they all agreed with his decision and so Reginald was happy at their response, saying that as he had found the boy he had done what he thought was best for him. The council told him that it was up to him what he did with his pseudo-apprentice and that they were sure that he had done the right thing.

Frank took the opportunity to say that the boy had been the best of them all for he had climbed a mountain to seek wisdom - and so seeing that they had lost the best candidate then it was not worth bothering with the rest. Then Arnold said that the lad had gone on a bit with that strange language of his. Frank leant backwards and closed his eyes indicating that he was beyond anything that Arnold could say or do to him.

"And he did fight a lot as well, so it was probably a good thing on the whole," added Arnold.

Frank smiled, saying that the inevitable had happened and it was only a question of time before the rest would go the same route. Jack promptly woke up to point out that if the boy were to fail with the priest then he would revert to them and would once more be Reginald's problem. On this note they disbanded, leaving Reginald telling Roger, "I... er... know of a few priests that would be able to deter that boy from his... um... idea of unworthiness and I can only hope that the one I chose is one... er... of them. Maybe he will be happy as an... umm... apprentice priest?"

"Well, I hope he is - for all our sakes, and you did well to find someone who would take him on."

Reginald smiled and sighed happily, saying, "Thank you Roger, he is now out of our hair, er... especially mine. And now, snack time - care to join me?" Roger nodded and Reginald asked, "Now, what shall we have?" Then they left to enjoy a celebratory mountain-boy-departure meal, or three.

Wilfred and his pupil were eating ice creams with things sticking out of them. Gloria swallowed another mouthful then asked, "Ingesting magic time?"

Admiring his latest food creation,[16] Wilfred lazily translated her words and saw that she thought it was time for her to learn more about magic. He turned his thought away from ice cream and towards thinking about the learning system that he was devising and the best way for her to memorize it. "Furrowed brows, stone clad words, ingest." (You will need to study and to memorize each lesson and spell exactly) he told her.

She continued digesting both the ice cream and his words (she found that she preferred his ice cream although his words were not too bad, so she accepted them as well). Finally, she told him, "Force taught ingest frozen but full I."

Trying not to spill what remained of his melting ice cream, Wilfred smiled and sucked in a lot of air, making his teeth go cold as he translated that she was full of ice cream and was now ready to start learning. Finally, he was able to say, "Copy fills you."

---

[16] Wilfred had added to the ice cream cones pieces of chocolate, banana bits, nuts, dolly mixtures, sherbet, liquorices of various shapes and lengths, icing, strawberries, and toast, and was now eating a combination of white and brown chocolate biscuits sprinkled with crushed almonds. Some of his early experiments had not worked very well especially the jam and - the worst mistake of all - cheese and onion!

Licking her fingers, she shrugged, indicating that she was ready whenever he was.

As casually as possible, he manifested *Book One of Becoming a Wizard* and handed it to her. She took it, gave it a long hard look, did the same at him, then back at the book, and then she nodded and went to find somewhere she could sit and read it, making Wilfred feel very happy.

Henry sat down heavily on the tree log and shook his head. He was not happy for he had a problem. His problem walked up to him, stood with his hands on his hips, and demanded that he learn some magic immediately. Once again, Henry tried to explain that it did not work like that. He started to explain about focalisation but Keryon stopped him saying he was talking about imagination again and he wanted to learn about real magic. Sighing deeply, Henry tried to get him to repeat one of the smallest and simplest spells that he knew. After only a few lines, the boy shook his head and moved away giving them both a much-needed break.

Henry was again tempted to use his magic to either force a change in attitude on his apprentice or to change him into something that was nicer to be around, like a kitten or a bag of fish and chips. Henry licked his lips at the thought of the fish and chips as he looked at his apprentice who was wandering around kicking the ground. He had tried many ways to get the young man engaged in the usual starting spells but he was either incapable or disinterested, or both. While Keryon was wandering back to stand in front of him, Henry briefly wondered how his fellow teachers were getting on with their particular adolescent pupils.

Henry stood slowly shaking his head, and said, "Things

were very different when I started." To his surprise, the boy looked at him in a questioning manner, so Henry explained, "When I was young, I had not shown any real gift or skill or interest for anything and as I was getting older and of no use something had to be found for me."

To his surprise, the boy asked, "So how old were you?"

Not looking at him Henry told him, "Ten summers, maybe twelve, when I started. They sent me for weeks at a time to various tradesmen and women in the hope that I would find a skill or at least enjoy the task. Nothing felt good or right to me; farming was dangerous, what with the animals and sharp tools everywhere. I was clumsy, shy, and timid and had little or no book learning and when I was left alone I just sort of sat thinking about things!"

The boy grinned and Henry saw him smile for the first time that day so he continued with his story, "It was the same with carpentry, or any kind of making - for I was dangerous with the tools - and them to me - and as I was shy I was no good at selling things or even talking to people. My distraught parents finally consulted the wise elder of our village. He told my father that I was no good with figures, not at all practical, and not able to communicate with people; he added that I was scared of most animals and when left alone I would go into daydreams. Just as the despair of my mother and relations was reaching a crescendo and threatening to drown me, the elder coughed and said that there were a couple of things that I just might be able to do. With my father's strong hands on my shoulders keeping me upright and stopping me from running away, the elder told us that I might be able to go into the dark arts. My mother said that I could not draw but he explained that what he meant by the dark arts were magicians and wizards. So I was sent to the nearest place where magic was performed - the local witch."

Henry saw that Keryon was really interested in his story and had sat down and was watching him. Smiling, he carried on, "This witch tested me, and then got me doing her housework while we waited for her message to get to the nearest male magic person. Just when I had broken most of her crockery and most of her patience, a tall dark man knocked and introduced himself as Clive the Wizard. He gave me a certain spell, then sent me outside to remember it while he and the witch discussed my fate. The spell was easy, short, and as the words rhymed, I was able to learn it in only half a day. That evening I said the spell to him and he showed me how to move my hands to the rhythm. Then I said it again and made a cloud of mist appear. I was despondent but they clapped their hands in joy saying that I had done well. Thus began my apprenticeship to becoming a wizard."

The boy had sat listening to him quietly and when the old man had finished, he asked how the spell went.

Smiling, Henry taught him the first spell he had learnt. It was a small beginning but one he knew they could build on. Happily, Henry suggested to the boy that it was time for a meal and he received a nod in response. So he suggested fish and chips and the boy gave another nod.

Henry later reported to the council that there might be a chance that this moody, arrogant, argumentative, nervous, insecure young man, who had no faith in himself and little in anything else, might just be able to get interested enough in some part of wizardry to find out if he was able to become a real 100% apprentice. The council told him that he was doing well and that he should do what he thought right with, and for, the boy.

Tom and Myrtle, the two farmers, were still doing most things together whenever they could, and if possible they did them looking into the other one's eyes. The exception was talking, for Tom did most of that while Myrtle just listened as she gazed deeply at him. All he talked about was farming and Myrtle, usually in that order. It had become obvious to every wizard - except for Frank who had gone away to sulk now that he could not find anyone who would listen to him complain. And it was not obvious to Albert (who was keeping out of the way) nor to Joe who had gone away to visit relatives (or so he had told everyone). Therefore, it was obvious to everyone, except for those who I have just mentioned, that Tom and Myrtle were not interested in becoming wizards in any shape, way, or form.

Tom and Myrtle were interested in only two things: each other and farming. All of their families had been farmers for as long as anyone could remember; they had been soaked in all things farm, farming, and farming mentality all of their lives so there was no room left anywhere for anything else. The wizards had offered to return them to one or the other of their families but as neither wanted to go to the other's land or be separated they had instead decided that they wanted to get married.

While the wizards were getting over this shock, Tom asked them if they could make them somewhere to live until they could get a small farm. After consulting his books, Francis decreed that there was nothing in any of his records that said there could not be farmers in Pearland - other than the fact that the soil was not very good and that it was windy, dry, and uninteresting, not to mention monotonous, stony, and boring. Pearland belonged as much to the wizards as to anybody else and if they wanted two farmers to stay so that they could start their married life together, then why not?

So the wizards spelled a priest (who kept on pinching his arm to see if he was dreaming) to perform the ceremony. Once he had married them, the priest was returned - via a forgetting spell - with black and blue bruises on his arm and a lot of money in his purse. Frank, who had got over his sulk about females not being able to become wizards and how this would be the end of them, now decided that he would have a better chance of winning an argument about the legality of the marriage.

He stated that if the priest could not remember anything then the wedding could not be legal. The rest of the council slowly faded away, wanting no part in the problem, leaving Frank, Arnold, and Roger deep in discussion.

Arnold argued that if the priest had died or lost his mind, then the weddings he conducted would still be valid.

"Is the priest dead? Has he lost his mind?" asked Frank and when Arnold told him that he was very much alive, as was his mind, Frank said that it didn't matter because he couldn't remember and so it was not legal. Roger asked him if he was suggesting that they should make the priest not alive or to lose his mind and, sneering, Frank replied that it would not make any difference for it still would not be valid. Arnold said that if the priest had remembered the wedding then he would tell people and then all sorts of people would be arriving to mess things up, and he would not like that one bit, then he added that they had the wedding paper thing as proof.

"The priest would not remember the wedding or us if you have taken away his memory."

Hiding his smile, Arnold said, "No one could forget us. Anyway, we are the last wizards left and that makes us unforgettable."

Nodding his head, Frank replied, "So if you forced him to forget, then he would forget the marriage as well and then it would not be legal - as I keep on saying!"

Roger sighed, then explained, "Frank - we have the piece of paper that he signed - and anyway we have been here before."

"We live here, Roger! Don't you remember?"

Snarling, Frank retorted, "You are impossible to talk with."

"You are more than impossible," added Arnold.

"That's impossible!" Frank replied without thinking.

"There! You see? I was right." Arnold said, closing his eyes in triumph.

Roger spoke, finally being able to get a word in, "Frank, I suspect that you are using language in a way that is not totally describing your true feelings and views on this subject. Am I right?"

Smiling and looking at Arnold, Frank replied, "You are so easy to wind up, Arnold! After all the times you have practiced directing your games at me, I thought it was time to teach you what it is like to be on the receiving end."

Arnold bowed as low as he could, saying, "Frank, coming from you, I like it very much... So, how do you feel about the priest?"

Grinning happily, Frank left Roger and Arnold to work it out; which Arnold did using only the digits of his left hand and one toe. Arnold smiled as he said. "Do you think Frank enjoyed that?"

"He seemed to," replied Roger, "but I wonder whether it was a `one off' or if he will join in all our little talks?"

"I doubt it somehow. How about a rest before the next council meeting?"

"Good idea, Arnold old chap."

That night Keryon and Mocker waited for the mountain boy, but he never showed. The next morning, they both asked their teachers where he was; and both teachers asked Reginald who explained that he had left. Mocker was very happy at the news, but not nearly as happy as Keryon whom Mountain Boy had used as a receiver of his fists. That night both boys tried to explain to each other that the mountain boy had gone. They managed eventually and both showed their happiness by smiling at each other for the first time.

At the next council meeting, the main issue was how to proceed with the farmers. They all agreed that if they sent them back to their respective relatives when they were in love and didn't want to go then the Law of Interference might come into play. They each made sounds or shuffled at the memories of when they had come against this before and quickly decided that the farmers might as well stay, as that was the least problematical solution to their problem. Satisfied that they had come up with a solution and had approved it, they looked around to find someone to receive the solution. They found Marcus, because he had brought Tom and because he was the easiest to get to do things.

Therefore, Marcus was told to go and give them

somewhere to live. So Marcus (being Marcus - full of guilt and feelings of inadequacy) took them for a walk so that they could select a place where he could spell them somewhere to live. Once they had decided on somewhere, Marcus spelled them a farmhouse, as this was what they were used to. He added a few animals, some tools and equipment although he did not know what they did to what where or why, as he had taken the images from their minds.

The two farmers felt as though they were in a sort of dream; they could not actually believe that this small, twitchy man could manifest all of these amazing things for them. Instead, they just kept on acting as if it were true, as that was the easiest. They finally said goodbye to Marcus and walked around their farmhouse touching the walls as if they would fade away. It would take them a very long time to come to terms with this and so they did what they knew best - they went to tend their animals.

Roger and Arnold were sitting, chatting pleasantly, when Arnold said that he was worried that people would come to Pearland.

"Why would people want to come here?" Roger asked innocently.

"To see where the strange farmers live."

"But there are farmers everywhere."

"Ahh... but these ones are different."

"Why are they different to any other farmers?" Roger asked, wondering where this was going.

"Because of us, of course. We are special."

Roger smiled. "Have you been talking to Frank?"

"Not talking to him - just practicing what I could say when I see him next. So, why don't you sum up things?"

Roger shook his head, and then grinned, before saying, "Well, each apprentice is going to be brought before us by the wizard who has undertaken their teaching."

"Rather them than me, what is next?"

"Reginald has taken his apprentice to become a priest."

"That might just suit him, what with his strange words and fighting."

"It was unusual for Reginald to be quite so decisive without consulting the council, don't you think?"

"Maybe, but it is very good for him as well. So the two farmers are to stay here, then?"

"Now it would seem so. Did you know that Marcus has spelled them a farm with all sorts of animals and things?"

"Frank will have plenty to say about that, I bet?"

"I am more than happy to forgo the experience of Frank's little chat until a later date."

"Suits me too, see him much later, right?"

"Oh yes, much later."

"So - all in all - things are quiet again?"

"Yes, until tomorrow - when we meet the apprentice candidates."

Grinning happily at the prospect, they sat in comfortable silence looking at the horizon in anticipation of the next day's events.

# *Chapter Fifteen: The Invitation*

The next morning the higher council arrived (with Arnold being the first of course). Each wizard looked at another wizard waiting to be told what to do next, for it had been a very long time since anything like this had happened. This looking at each other and waiting continued until someone asked, "Should we not have somewhere to interview them rather than out in the middle of nowhere?" The wizards all turned and looked at Colin as they tried to remember what the word 'interview' meant.

Arnold explained, "We might need a room or something to see them in - out of the wind - where we can tell them that they are accepted, if they are that is."

Roger nodded and looked at each of the wizards until he came to Frank who said, "Why not build them a house to live in as well?"

Ignoring the sarcasm, Arnold replied, "What a good idea! Maybe with two rooms - one for the boys and one for the girls - but I see that we have these already... so maybe we should just have somewhere to tell them they have been accepted?"

Frank folded his arms in disgust and turned his back on the discussion. So it was agreed that first they would spell a fitting place to see the apprentices and then not to spell somewhere for the apprentices to sleep.

While Frank was saying that sarcasm was the lowest form

of wit, Arnold spelled a large tall oblong building with two doors at each end and three windows on each side. Then the wizards went inside and discussed on what and where they should sit. They finally agreed that a tiered seat with a small wooden front was best with a flat area for Jack's settee. They settled themselves down only after discussing who should be near the front or back and only then were they ready to see the first child who wanted to become a wizard's apprentice.

Joe (who had found Myrtle) and Albert (who had found Mocker) were not going to attend as their two candidates had either married or was going to be trained by Bill as he knew sign language. They were very happy about losing their apprentices while Marcus was not, for he felt that he had failed again even though he had spelled a huge farm complete with animals for Tom and Myrtle. Reginald, who had taken his boy to a priest, was also free from attending the interviews and was having a nice sausage sandwich and a cup of coffee instead. So the first wizard to bring forward an applicant was Wilfred with Gloria.

They entered the large hall blinking to help their eyes adjust to the dimness after the morning sunshine. They walked over until they were standing before the assembled wizards and looked around. Roger asked them to come and stand in front of them if they would not mind. They stood in front of the higher council, the small blonde yellow-bearded wizard quietly whispering to the girl with the multi coloured hair in kid-speak.

Roger coughed to get their attention and when they were both looking at him, told them, "The Extended Council of Wizards welcomes you, miss. So, tell us a little about yourself, could you? And why you would like to become a wizard?"

The girl looked up at Wilfred who smiled encouragingly so she shrugged and told them, "Sow sold me to wiz after putting me into kid-cage. Wiz unrolls me infill about unbuckle and treeless."

The wizards looked at each other blankly, then at Wilfred who asked the child if he could interpret for her. Again she shrugged so he told them, "Her mother sent her to a boarding school to get her out of the way. She was really unhappy there so when I offered her the option of being put forward she jumped at the chance. I went to see her mother who took some money for her and signed a piece of paper making me her guardian. She wants to be free to choose what she does without the constrictions that she has so far spent her life under."

Arnold chuckled while Frank shook his head and folded his arms in disgust. Francis sat nodding, appreciating some of the way that she used words; Colin made notes on his clipboard that Douglas tried to read over his shoulder, and Jack slept on. Roger nodded in agreement then said, "The Extended Council of Wizards is privileged to offer you an apprenticeship. You will train mainly under Wilfred, but also maybe other wizards, until the time comes when you are either made into a fully-fledged wizard or are asked to leave or leave of your own accord. Does this suit you Miss... ah... Miss...?"

"Gloria is my known bye." Wilfred glanced at her as she continued, "Thank you, Wizards Council, very much topping." She then turned to Wilfred who glanced at the council and gave them a quick smile before leading her away.

Arnold waited until they were out of sight before saying, "That was not too bad now, was it?"

Frank shook his head, saying "It's the first nail in the coffin of our demise, is what it is."

"She certainly has an unusual manner about her," said Colin.

"Her hair is unusual as well - not as I remember women's hair used to look," said Arnold.

Douglas adjusted his glasses, thinking of something else entirely; Roger watched Jack who opened his left eye, used it to look at him then gave a slight nod before closing it again, indicating that he agreed that she was an excellent choice for a candidate.

Outside the building, Wilfred and Gloria slapped their right hands against each other in various places and each time they connected hands, they made a slapping sound to show that they were happy. Afterwards they discussed what had just happened. "Wrinklies really wizzers?" she asked (Are those old wrinkled men really amazing wizards?)

"They are wiz filled and pruned out cos they over lived." (Those fine old gentlemen are the best and finest wizards that there has ever been and are much wrinkled because they have lived much longer than most).

She looked at him, then slowly allowed her mouth to change into a smile; then she grabbed her waist and jumped up and down in the air. Wilfred watched her for a moment until he worked out that was her way of showing extreme joy and excitement, so he copied her actions and soon they were both laughing so much that they had to stop.

When they had both finally stopped jumping up and down and could again talk, she asked, "Glue us you infill me wiz and not break or bend?" (We are going to spend our time together with you showing me how to become a wizard, but you will not hurt me or be cruel to me in any way, will you?)

Wilfred gasped at the very idea and she saw from his face that he was shocked, so she smiled and apologised, but he told her, "If I ever start to bend or break you even with a heavy sound then you tell wrinkly wizzers and they break me, right?" (If I ever threaten you with any form of violence, including shouting or being mean, then you go to the council and inform them and they will reprimand me, okay?)

She nodded, then grinned and then started to jump up and down again and soon Wilfred was doing the same.

Henry then brought in the youth he had rescued from the monastery and stood with him in front of the council. Roger made the same speech[17] (except he added 'young man' instead of 'miss') and then he waited for the boy to say something.

Keryon stood trying to look brave and unconcerned as he replied, "I am from a poor village that can only support those who can do the most for the most, and I am not that good. They are forced to send out anyone who is not as good as the rest. This year it was my turn. I was sent to wait in front of the monks' home to see if I would be taken in, but as I waited I got angry and then he came up...," He pointed at Henry who nodded in agreement, "...all nice and dry and us all wet - and I lost my temper. He said he could bring me here to see if I would be accepted - and so long as I am

---

[17] "The Higher Council of Wizards welcome you, miss. (I did say that he changed this miss to young man, remember?) So, tell us a little about yourself, could you? And why you would like to become a wizard?"

treated right then I want to do it. Okay?"

The council hid their smiles, except for Frank who scowled, and Jack who snored loudly, leaving Roger to say, "The Extended Council of Wizards is privileged to offer you an apprenticeship. You will start your training under Henry, but this could change and you might also train with other wizards as well or instead. This will continue until the time comes when you are either made into a fully-fledged wizard, are asked to leave or leave of your own accord. Does this suit you... er... young man?"

Henry said that his name was Keryon then he winked at Keryon reminding him to reply to the offer of a wizard's apprenticeship. "Yeah, ta. I mean... I thank you for the chance and I will do my best. Thank you, Sirs." Then he and Henry left the building.

When they were out of sight, Arnold was the first to speak, "He was very polite for one so young, most unusual." Douglas looked at him to see if he was being sincere or sarcastic.

"And he seemed to see our offer as something valuable," Francis added.

"You can never tell," said Frank "I thought the boy looked shifty and he was not really that polite."

"It takes one to know one - but then he does look a lot like you, come to think of it."

"You beat me to it there, Arnold," smiled Roger.

"Good, that means that I was the first, Roger. I must admit he does seem to have the right spirit and manners - and they have never hurt anyone. So, who is next?"

Outside, Henry stood talking to Keryon. "So how does it feel to be a fully accepted apprentice?" The boy blinked before replying that it felt good but a bit hungry. Laughing, Henry said that he would spell them some food that was good enough for a working wizard's apprentice and Keryon jutted out his jaw indicating that his offer would be acceptable.

Bill strolled into the hall with the girl with the muscles beside him. She was still wearing the same odd garment with faded letters and numbers on it. Bill had offered to spell her something else but she told Bill she wanted to keep it until she had either been accepted or rejected. Tara stood looking defiantly up at the higher council but they could see that she was very scared underneath her public image of defiance.

Bill introduced her as Tara then stood protectively at her side, leaving Roger to give his speech, "Hallo there. We, of the Extended Council of Wizards, welcome you, Tara. It is very nice to meet you and we hope that you are well. Could you please tell us why you would like to become a wizard?"

She looked into his eyes then did the same with the rest of the council (except for Jack who seemed to be sleeping). Jack was not looking at her with his eyes but he still felt her pain and silently spelled the ability for her to start healing and recover from at least some of her many ordeals. As she briefly held their eyes, each wizard saw and felt that she was a very scared, and a very scary, young female who had been through unimaginable traumas and had survived mostly intact. Frank saw her as frightening on many levels and quickly looked away. Francis acknowledged that she was someone out of his experience and knew that he would never have been able to survive what she had gone through. Douglas thought that she was a poor wee lassie who needed to find someone to trust. Arnold saw through the anger a glimpse of her kindness and nodded at her as he ignored her imposing physique. Colin saw her strength and resolve, felt humbled in her presence, and did not even think of her as one of his cases. Roger held her eyes as he sent towards her as much honesty as he had about himself at this time, for he sensed that was what she deserved.

She nodded at Roger as she told them that she wanted to find a way to be able to live without any restraints on her freedom so that she could live in whichever way was right for her.

Roger bowed slightly forward before telling her, "That is a very good reason, as good as any. As wizards, we do have more freedom than most - but not as much as you might think - but then, maybe more than you can imagine. I would like to offer you the position of wizard's apprentice where you would be working with Bill to begin with. There may be others as well, or maybe even instead, who may teach you if things indicated that this would be the right thing to do. This may be because Bill, we, or maybe even you, might decide that you need a change. This will be done with respect to you, as I am sure that you will come to respect us who will treat you accordingly. The position will last until you become a fully-fledged wizard, if you decide to leave for some reason, or if we ask you to leave. Do you understand what I have just said?"

She stood looking up into his eyes holding her body tense as she said that she did and would do her best as long as things were fair and good. Roger nodded at her and waited for her to leave with Bill.

Instead, Bill coughed to get his and as much of the

council's attention as possible. Then he informed them that the next candidate was the boy called Mocker and that he wondered if Tara could stay and help with interpreting their and Mocker's words. Roger looked around him while Frank muttered that this was very unusual and no one bothered to point out that having apprentices in any form was also highly unusual. Jack wheezed in his sleep (or maybe it was a laugh, Arnold did not know which).

"I say we should give this deaf boy as much chance as we can and if this girl who can hand talk is willing and able to help him, then why not?" said Arnold. Colin nodded in agreement, watching Tara and still thinking that he would not have survived even a week as a slave. Frank said that it did not matter anyway for they were all doomed; and Roger told him that as it did not matter then they would do what they wanted - making Frank purse his lips and fold his arms in disdain. Douglas shrugged, indicating that he had no strong opinions on the subject and Francis grinned, saying that he wanted to see more of this hand talking so that he could write about it. So Roger turned back to Bill and said that the council had decided that, on this one occasion, they would consent.

Tara frowned, wondering what was going on while Bill told her that he would go and get Mocker and that she should stay where she was. She folded her arms and glared at the roof, making some of the wizards (Frank, Colin, and Arnold) feel nervous. Roger spelled a chair and offered it to her. She stared at it in disbelief and then said that he was very kind but she would rather stand if he didn't mind. Roger, who was only trying to be kind, saw that she didn't think that any chair suddenly produced out of thin air would be able to take her weight, so he inclined his head, showing that he understood.

Bill soon returned with a small boy dressed in green and brown garments that were too big for him. He did not want anything new until he knew if he was accepted or not, just like Tara. These baggy overalls were normal for a person of the forest, while being deaf was not.

Roger coughed, then remembered that the boy could not hear him, so he asked Bill, "How does he understand what is being said to him?"

Bill looked down at the child, then back at Roger, saying, "Why not ask him - and that?"

Roger bit back his retort that he didn't know how to address him which was why he was asking; instead, he stared at the small figure and said, "Hallo there... how do I communicate with you?"

Tara moved to stand in front and to one side of Mocker and watched as he made signs with his hands towards her. She turned and explained, "He can read some words on people's lips, but you wizards all have hairy lips so he finds it difficult, but I can tell him what you say."

Douglas idly wondered if he should point out that he alone did not have either a beard or a moustache and then forgot it as he watched the proceedings. "We of the Extended Council of Wizards welcome him. Can you tell us... I mean... why does he want to be a wizard?" said Roger.

The higher council watched as Tara moved her hands and head towards the boy who made signs back, and then she signed again using more signs. After the boy had watched her he said to Roger in an odd croaky voice, "Wizard me want so I do what I want."

"He wants freedom like me," Tara added "so that he doesn't have to do what others tell him or force him to do something."

Roger nodded and glanced at the rest of the council; Frank was sitting with folded arms, shaking his head and muttering quietly; Colin was leaning forward, watching the young couple intently. Douglas was sitting with his head cocked to one side and tapping his lips with his index finger; Jack had one eye open looking at the hand-moving couple. Francis was watching with wide open eyes, his lips moving silently as he wrote down in his mental diary as many of their actions as he was able to understand. Arnold was frowning with concentration and wrinkles and Roger said, "That is fine and a very good reason. Thank you." He stood waiting while Tara translated then he said to her, "We, of the Extended Council of Wizards..."

Tara who was watching Mocker turned and told him, "Hey... look at him, not me."

Roger blinked a couple of times then saw how impolite he was being by not talking or looking at the boy but at Tara who was only translating. He apologised then continued, "Mocker, we of the Higher Council of Wizards would like to offer you the chance to become an apprentice - working mostly with Bill - but you might also have to work with others, and perhaps even instead, if circumstances so decide."

He paused as Tara asked him what 'circumstances' meant. He scratched his head as he explained, "Well, we might think that Bill is not doing as well as some other wizard might do, or Bill might want a change, or someone might have a specialisation in some particular subject... I mean different things to teach you... that they might know more about than Bill." He again paused, allowing Tara to catch up but she stood waiting so he shook his head, wondering how this hand talking worked as he said, "This will continue until you leave, until we ask you to leave, or until you become a fully-fledged wizard. So, does he have any questions?"

Tara translated as best she could but she knew that she had not really put across half of what the words really meant so she turned to Bill and explained her worries. Bill stood with his hands on his stomach, nodding, and then turned to the council and said that he intended to spell the information to Mocker to make sure that he understood. Before anybody could say anything he quickly spelled an information spell that explained everything that Roger had said plus much more (such as how Roger's voice had gone up and down and what 'circumstances' meant).

Mocker stood gulping air until the spell had finished its course. Then he stood, nodding, and said thank you in his unused voice.

Bill turned back to face the higher council and said, "The boy now understands what is being offered to him. What he wants is freedom, as I'm sure you would if you were in his position - and that."

Roger nodded, as did Colin, Francis, and Arnold, while Douglas said that out of all of them, he needed the help that the knowledge of wizards could give him. Jack grunted in his sleep, leaving Roger to thank Mocker and to wish him well, whatever happened. Bill looked at his two apprentices and asked them if they were ready to leave. Tara nodded while Mocker bowed at the council before thanking them, and then nodded.

When they had left the building, Douglas said that he could not imagine how hard it must be not to be able to hear anything. Francis said that if he had never heard then it would not mean the same as if he had lost his hearing, which in many ways might be worse or easier. Douglas said that either way it must be so hard, then he said that he was very impressed just how much the hand moving was able to convey.

Colin silently wondered how being deaf would change the basic mental thinking process and about the effects on the person's identity; and concluded that if a person had been born deaf and found a way of communicating, then they might not see this condition as a disability, just a basic part of their identity. He then thought that the personalities of those who could not hear might be just like everybody else's. He also wondered if a deaf person used sign language to communicate when they dreamed or whether they could hear in their dreams.

"The kid has guts - no matter how you look at it," said Arnold and most of the council agreed, with the exception of Jack (who said nothing), and Frank, who said that having a deaf person in charge of spells and wizards's knowledge was a recipe for complete disaster and that things could not get any worse. Roger raised his hand, stopping Arnold and Douglas's response as he said, "He is now an apprentice and it is up to him, and Bill, and maybe even Tara, as to what happens with the chance that we have offered him."

"I just hope we will all be alive to see our mistake," muttered Frank.

The council sat looking at the door waiting for the next

applicant. After a while, Frank asked if they were being treated with the respect they deserved, by having to wait so long.

Before any of the council could reply, the tall solid form of Martin entered. He was taking very small steps to keep the same speed as his companion, a short, fat, round chubby child with a shock of bright red hair and a face full of spots. They slowly came to a stand in front of the council. She clung onto the tall wizard's hand as if she might drown without it and clutched a teddy bear under her arm. Martin smiled at the council as he explained that they had to make a couple of stops for she had got tired and needed to drink quite a lot, and once to lose some of her liquid.

Arnold frowned, wondering what he meant; Francis wondered if her whole family had had the same hair colour; Colin looked at the fat child and wondered if she had arrested development and if she was really as young as she looked and if the shape of her face was due only to fat or if it was an indication that she might have some form of brain damage. Frank smiled at seeing that she was still a baby and that there was no chance of making her into a wizard and shivered happily as he imagined her with having spells to turn people into lollipops, or worse. Jack snored quietly; Arnold thought it was a shame that she had no parents; Douglas hoped that he wouldn't have to encounter her in any way, as he was not good with babies.

Roger wondered if she could talk as he said, "Welcome there, little miss. Now, what's your name?"

The child turned and hugged Martin's leg, leaving Martin to explain that her name was Follia and that she was a bit shy.

Roger frowned and rocked gently backward and forward as he asked, "So why does she want to become a wizard?" Martin gently rubbed the vivid red hair of his charge and asked her if she wanted to talk to the nice man.

She turned and said, "Want him." Then she hid her head against Martin's knee as Roger shook his head, wondering if she understood any of what was going on. Martin got down on his knees and held the child out just in front of him as he tried to explain that the nice man had to be looked at or she might have to go back. The child immediately burst into tears, making a loud squealing noise to accompany them.

Frank threw his hands up in the air[18] as he shook his head and made odd noises, supposedly to indicate that he was beyond shock, but instead only sounding like he really needed to leave the room. Slowly the red-haired girl's crying turned into sobs then slowly subsided altogether. She turned her head until she could peek around Martin's leg to see the large round form of Roger. Roger did not know what to do, so he waved at her. To his surprise, she giggled and hid her face again. This turned into a long game of peek-a-boo that made Frank turn his back on the proceedings in disgust.

Soon Follia was smiling at Roger, and he then, in a very gentle voice, asked why she wanted to stay with Martin.

"Nice man give me food," she replied.

Douglas remembered her history, that she had come from a castle where her parents had abandoned her to a sort of children's home. Roger looked around at the council to see if anybody had anything to say. When he saw that only Frank had many things to say he turned back to the child

[18] It was all right - for they were still attached to his wrists, so there was no chance of him losing them.

saying, "We of the Wizards Council offer you a place to learn and be safe with Martin until you want to leave, or we ask you to leave or until you become a fully functioning wizard."

"When that day comes it will be raining frogs and flowers," muttered Frank, but everyone ignored him again.

Martin asked Follia what she had to say to the nice man. She looked up at him, then back at Roger saying, "Thank yoo. Me wanna stay him." Then she shrugged and looked down at her new shoes.

Roger rolled his shoulders for something to do, then said, "That is good enough for me, and I wish you all the best."

She nodded at him wisely, "I got noo shoes... and socks... look!" she told him before Martin led her out of the room, leaving the wizards to discuss the possibility of any baby being able to learn wizardry.

Martin stopped outside of the structure that they had just left for Follia was getting tired from walking all the way to the room, and then standing and walking all the way back outside again. He asked her if she was hungry and, to his surprise, she said that she was not. So instead, he spelled a large soft settee for them to sit on until she had recovered. He wondered if the fact that she had refused food for the first time was a good sign or if it indicated that she was not well. He smiled as he sat holding her tiny hand in his large, capable one.

Back inside the interview room, Frank was saying how dangerous it was to give a baby any spell knowledge. Arnold disagreed and said that Martin knew a thing or two, and then Colin duly added that they seemed to have bonded. Frank said that was nothing for she was like a beaten animal that would respond to any kindness; and Roger said that was just like most things; leaving Frank to say that it would all end in annihilation if not worse. Francis asked what was worse than annihilation, and then asked if eradication was worse, extinction, or even obliteration, adding that they all described much the same thing, meaning the end in a most dramatic way. Frank said that he could mock but they would all see that he right, but by then it would be too late; leaving Francis to wonder why Frank had thought that he had been mocking him.

Arnold had been sitting with a smug smile on his face until Roger asked him what he was smiling about.

"I am smiling because we now have five, did you hear me? five apprentices - and so out of them we should get at least two wizards."

"The odds you are calculating seem to be on the high side, and might not include all of the factors that could prohibit the success rate," said Colin.

Frank got to his feet and said in a loud agitated voice, "Out of the five we might get two! Are you mad?" Getting to his feet he continued, "We have five youths who have all had really unhappy lives, one is still a baby, and each of them have problems with talking with the exception of one poor lad who was chased out of his village by his family. They all have big problems with everything, talking being only one of them - and did I mention that three of them are girls?..."

Before Frank could continue with his tirade, Roger stood up and stopped his words, saying loudly, "Thank you Frank. I think that we all know how you feel about the situation. So, does anybody else have anything else to say?"

Arnold said that he was more than happy that they had five - he looked at Frank as he repeated - FIVE apprentices in an even louder voice.

Then Douglas said, "Aye... What aboot them farmers?"

"Oh... I'd completely forgotten about them," said Roger.

"Where are they?" Colin asked.

"Marcus has spelled them a farm..." replied Arnold.

Before Frank could expel his thoughts and feelings on the subject, someone asked, "So, what we gonna do with them?"

"Good question there, Douglas my man," said Roger. "If we part them then we break the Law of Interference, so we will leave them on their farm. As we all know nothing grows here, they will voluntarily move away, thus not causing us to break any laws."

Frank almost screamed as he said, "You have spelled them a FARM? Of all things! My mind boggles."

"What you do in the privacy of your own mind is your own business," retorted Arnold.

Then Colin said that as they had spelled a farm for them it would be most interesting to see how the farmers would mentally adjust to not being able to grow things. The discussion went on for some time until Jack opened his right eye and said, "The best option we have is to give them a chance. No matter how small a chance it is all that we can do after bringing them away from what they know."

The council looked at each other until they ran out of looks and then Roger asked them what they all thought. Colin said that it would be good to witness their behaviour; Douglas said that no matter how bad things were they at least had each other (making the council look at him with new eyes[19]). Francis said that out of the two options spelling a farm was the least consequential.

"It might be nice to have a farm around..." said Arnold "...something to look at with our new eyes, perhaps?" he suggested, looking at Frank.

"Have you really spelled a farm?" In disbelief, Frank repeated the words, "A FARM!"

Roger scratched the back of his left ear and looked at the ground as he told Frank that they already had. Frank made sounds as he eyes got larger and his arms waved around.

Roger turned to the rest of the council, telling them that Marcus had indeed spelled them a farm and would spell whatever else they needed to survive, until they left.

"Not only are we going to doom ourselves with girls and children who cannot communicate - with all kinds of attitude problems," said Frank "...but you're also going to mess up the area by spelling a farm and all that entails to go with it!" He slapped his forehead, saying that he now had heard it all, and that he gave them six months at the most, for this was the end of them all. Colin smiled at Frank who, not knowing how to respond, just shook his head, then disappeared away to his room to sulk and worry. Colin then started to think that what Frank needed was his *worst scenario protection* that he used to keep himself safe from what he imagined could be worse than any reality. He nodded goodbye to Arnold and Roger and went to his room where he spent a long time looking in his textbooks to find who originally came up with the *worst scenario protection* theory.

---

[19] I know that I said that they had ran out of looks but they were wizards, remember, so could look at things with their attitude as well as their eyes, so they just spelled new ones.

Douglas explained that he would drop Jack off on the way to his room and then did just that.

Arnold looked around at the empty (except for him and Roger) room and sighed, confessing that he had really enjoyed the meeting. Roger scratched his head then said he had as well.

Arnold looked up at the roof of his spelled building saying, "This is not bad, you know. I quite like it."

Roger nodded then said, "That is that then... if you listen to Frank."

"Well, it might not be..." Arnold moved his wrinkles around as he replied.

"What do you mean?" Roger asked him.

Smiling and again looking up at the roof, he said, "It might be the end - or it might just be the beginning. It depends on others, I suspect."

"Arnold, old man, you are very wise," nodded Roger in agreement.

Now you get to decide whether Arnold or Frank is right.

**The New Beginning**

# WAY OF THE WIZARDS

## NEW BEGINNINGS

### Book Two

The wizards of Pearland have managed to find some young apprentices, but the apprentices cannot communicate and spend most of their time fighting with each other. It gets so bad that the wizards must find a child minder to control them when they are not being trained. But then the child minder needs a shop so that she can buy her female things, and nobody can be found to open a shop, since there are no paying customers in Pearland. The wizards try to attract paying customers by bringing in a dragon's egg but then things start to get complicated.

Available April 2012 worldwide in print and eBook formats.

ISBN: **9781590957295**

# Way Of The Wizards

## Arrivals New & Old

### Book Three

Fifteen wizards, who long ago moved to a barren, distant land called Pearland in order to practice their wizardry in peace, have now accumulated a group of young apprentices as well as a child minder. A shy female dragon then decides to join them. Later, out of boredom, one wizard decides to cover the ground in a smooth, slab-like substance in the hope that it might entice travellers. And it does, in ways that nobody could have anticipated.

Available October 2012 worldwide in print and eBook formats.

"I love this book. The story and the characters stay with me, resonating and mirroring different parts of me that at times feel challenging and at others tickle. I was not ready for it to end, I'm still not, and eager for its sequel."

-- *China Hunter, founder/owner/muse, Cafe del Soul*

This book will make you laugh, shout, cry, or irritate the hell out of you – you might even make a few wizard friends – it might even change your life.

-- *Peter Fricker, Energy Healer, founder Energy Remedy, UK*

"It's a book about wizards in a fantasy world but everywhere I looked I kept seeing things from my past and present in a way that reminds me of The Tao of Pooh but even more playful and while not trying to be a book on the psychology of relationships.

-- *Bruce Barstow, Fantasy Fan and Technical Instructor*

Lightning Source UK Ltd.
Milton Keynes UK
UKOW051339091211

183478UK00001B/8/P